Jane and Bingley:

Austen in Love #2

by Jenni James

JANE & BINGLEY —

Austen in Love #2
Countdown to Christmas
by Jenni James

Other books in the Austen in Love series:
My pride His Prejudice
Persuaded

This book is dedicated . . .

To all the fans who emailed and begged for this closure—here it is, the story of Jane and Charles. I hope you love it as much as I have. Thank you for letting me repent and experience this with you. It was so much fun! And you were right—it was needed.

To Chloe—my heart bled for you as I wrote this, but it gave me the strength to believe in happiness again. I love you, sweetie.

CHAPTER ONE
On the First Day of Christmas

It was the Christmas wedding of the year—December 23rd. Simply everyone who was anyone was there. Jane glanced around the room for what seemed like the hundredth time that night. She swirled the rum-free eggnog in her pretty fluted wineglass and sighed. Her silver holiday dress—the one she spent a fortune on at Macy's—sparkled under the white fairy lights draped above her. There was laughter and joyous celebration all around. Everyone had come to her sister, Eliza's, wedding to Will Darcy. It was the most-anticipated and talked-about party this season, full of hope and happiness.

Except she wasn't hopeful, and she wasn't happy. Well—for herself. For Eliza, she couldn't be happier. No two people were more in love, or more ready for marriage than they were. And up until this moment—this exact past hour—it had been such a whirlwind of months and months of planning. Of contacting caterers and auditioning dresses, for that's really what trying on wedding dresses is— auditioning the very best one for the big day. Consulting hair, floral, photographers, caterers… the list went on and on. For what seemed like forever, this had been their biggest concern, and all that was talked about in the Bennet household.

Now it was over. Or almost over.

Jane rose her glass with the several others who applauded and sipped another toast to the couple. She wasn't paying much attention. Her toast was finished long ago, and with it was shed many tears of delight for her sister. But now… now there was nothing. Her last big part of the evening was over, and all that was left was a perfectly coiffed hairstyle, a glittering gown, and an empty seat next to her.

Her heart dropped as she finally glanced over to the calligraphy-written name card at her right. Charles Bingley. He hadn't come. After all his promises and those silly texts and emails assuring her they had much to talk about and to make up for lost time—all of that—it was over. He made it clear that not only did he not have time for his friend's wedding, but for the sister of the bride, either.

Jane's hand shook slightly, and she set the wineglass down. During the next applause, she stood up and carefully made her way through throngs of tables to the hallway of the elaborate rented building. If it wasn't for her dang heels, she would've taken the steps a bit quicker. She was almost to the restroom when she passed by a large darkened ballroom—one of its ornate French doors had been left open. It obviously had not been rented that evening. The empty room was too tempting to pass up. She needed a few minutes of peace and quiet to pull herself together, and what better place than an abandoned ballroom?

She slipped inside and allowed her eyes to adjust to the dark as she trailed the paneled wall with her fingertips. It was a little over a year ago that she and Charles had actually met. A year since she was immediately blown head over heels. He was perfect—they were perfect—or so she thought. Everything came crashing down a few months later when he was assigned to open new offices in New York. It was then that Charles took her to lunch and told her it just wasn't going to work out. That being so far apart would put a strain on their relationship, and they needed to take a break.

That was eight months ago.

Eight long, ridiculous months.

She knew she was being impractical to even fall for someone she hardly knew, but then to still miss him eight months later was absurd! Honestly, what was wrong with her? She should've known that the first chance he had, he'd break her hope again. Yes, it was hope—not heart. She refused to acknowledge that her heart had been broken or would be broken by him again.

The stillness of the dark room seemed to envelop her as she walked farther into it. This was exactly what she craved—alone time. Being away from the bustling excitement. She had to process and take a few moments for herself before she came back.

So he had said months ago that they shouldn't date anymore. Lately, he'd been messaging, saying he'd missed her and was wrong and would like to start again. But with her hectic schedule—work and last-minute errands for the wedding, and his frantic New York schedule, they had yet to actually meet up. It was supposed to be tonight.

As in, a few hours ago. Which is why she'd splurged and purchased the silly dress and went all out on her makeup and hair and had butterflies in her stomach all day. Knowing he'd be watching her in front of everyone, during the ceremony, and really seeing her for the first time in months. It was nerve-racking and irrational all at the same time.

She couldn't find him in the massive crowd of people who had come, but she figured he would approach her. When he didn't, she rationalized the fact that Eliza had made sure he was sitting right next to her. If all else failed, she would definitely see him at dinner. But it failed. He wasn't there.

Her chest tightened, and she straightened her back before she let the panic of her stupidity overwhelm her. So what? So what if Charles didn't show up? What did it matter to her? Nothing. He was nothing. And he would continue to be nothing. She had no patience for players, anyway. Besides, there was probably a very good reason why he didn't make the wedding. Like, twenty of them, but why he did or didn't come shouldn't matter to her one bit. She took a deep breath and attempted not to overreact. The fact she was actually away from the crowd and hiding in an empty room proved she was being dramatic.

There was no drama here. None.

It was time to head back to the reception and smile and laugh and help where she could. Heaven knew, her mother was probably a nervous wreck, looking for her. Jane took a deep breath, turned toward the open door, and then froze. There he was. Standing in the room. His face was in shadow, but she would recognize his frame anywhere.

"Sorry. Forgive me. I didn't mean to startle you." Charles took a step toward her and then stopped. "I saw you leave and followed you in here."

"You—you did?" Her voice nearly cracked.

"Yes. You were so deep in thought, I didn't want to disturb you. Should I come back another time? We can definitely catch up later."

Jane's breathing was so erratic, she was positive he could see her heart pounding through her dress. He came. He actually came. And he'd followed her in here to talk to her. "When did you get to the wedding?"

"Just before the ceremony. I was running late and then got caught up with friends and family and was forced to sit with them during dinner. I know we were supposed to sit together, but . . . um… How are you? Are you okay?" He took another step forward.

For the first time, Jane Bennet actually had the urge to snap. He had been here the whole time? Since the ceremony over two hours ago, and he hadn't even come up and said hello? He was "caught" with family? And yet, he knew she was alone and waiting for him? Even if they were viable excuses, something about them seemed pretty lame.

If this was supposed to be their chance to start over, a whole lot needed to change. And it would have to be her who implemented it. She slowly walked toward him until they were nearly face-to-face in her heels. Then she slipped a hand under his tie and pulled him toward her. Gently, her lips met his for the first time in months. His faint cologne surrounded her.

She smiled as she felt him gasp and then released her hold. "Welcome back, Charles. I hope your flight went well." Their eyes met in the darkened room, and she let one eyebrow rise slightly. "I guess I'll see you around." Then she turned—before she lost her nerve—and walked out into the brightly lit hallway.

"Wait." He caught up with her as she headed back to the reception.

"Yes?"

It was as if he didn't know what to do. "Are you mad at me?"

"Nope." Her pace quickened as she smiled. "I'm happy to see you."

"And the kiss?"

She paused and glanced up at him. "Just a welcome home." She fiddled with the diamond watch at her wrist. "Look, I'm sorry. I've got to get back and help my family with everything. It was great seeing you."

Charles's jaw dropped. "Are you kidding? I thought we'd get to talk or something. You know, discuss *us*?"

Jane shrugged as she began to walk again. "Pity. So did I." She was clearly not his top priority—the fact that she had made him hers was enough. If he really wanted to put things right and get back together, he needed to step up his game.

She might still be the nicest girl he'd ever known, but she wasn't willing to be tossed aside again. He needed to realize her worth, or this relationship was over before it began. This time, Jane Bennet would be courted, acknowledged, seen, and cared about. She wanted a real man.

And she had every intention of getting him.

CHAPTER TWO

My True Love Gave to Me

Charles stomped his snow-covered shoes on the mat as he came into the house later that night. What a waste of a good evening! He shivered as he flipped on the lights and crossed the hall to the thermostat. After setting his suitcases down, he fiddled with the little contraption until the heater clicked on. How long had it been since he was home? A month? Two?

The place smelled stale and unused. And cold. Yeesh, it was frigid. He rubbed his hands together as he walked into the small kitchen, searching for something to warm himself with until the walls decided to thaw out. In a bottom cupboard, he found an old kettle, filled it up, and placed it on the stove to whistle at him when it was done. Then after a few vain attempts of looking in empty cupboards, he finally found the tin of hot cocoa that had been stashed above the oven for safekeeping last year. Even it was cold as he attempted to remove the tight lid. Once it was open, he put some spoonfuls into a mug.

Then he waited.

And waited.

Why did it take so long for water to boil?

He pushed off from the counter and instead went to unpack his luggage. He had told the New York team that he was taking a month off, and anything urgent could be sent via email. Revolutionary Innovations was soaring in the Big Apple, even bigger than he or Will Darcy could've predicted eight short months ago. Will's designs were incredible and definitely needed in today's ever-changing market. With a New York address, the company was able to get noticed worldwide as a leader in technology and advancements. He knew that office needed him, but sometimes enough was enough.

After Will and Eliza's honeymoon was over, the couple had promised to head out to New York and stay there, covering anything necessary and enjoying the bright lights while Charles took a much-needed break back home.

He rubbed the back of his neck and hauled the first suitcase into his bedroom as he flicked on the light. It felt good to be able to say he'd be here longer than a weekend. To get to spend the holidays with family and Jane ... His brain sort of stopped right there. He couldn't think of anything else but her. Why had she acted so weird that night? Was it just him, or did she not seem that eager to see him? Had Eliza and Will broken their promise not to tell her anything until he could explain? He sat down on the bed and stared at nothing in particular for a moment.

He had no one to blame but himself. Sure, he'd wanted to punch Will the second the man confessed he'd been wrong all along and Jane actually liked him—*and* she wasn't just after his money. But in all honesty, *he* was the one who fell for it. He knew Jane better, knew she was the exact girl he'd always wanted by his side. He was the one who panicked at the first rumor and jumped ship, not Will. He didn't have to listen to Will's opinions. That choice was all on Charles.

Why had he panicked? Why ruin a sure thing? Those questions had been haunting him for days now, and the only thing he could think of was that perhaps things were moving too fast and he just wasn't ready for her. So he was looking for an excuse—anything to stop the scariness of actually finding *the one* and settling down.

Settling down. He took a deep breath and lay back on his pillow. Was he willing to rethink and restart his life? He shook his head and closed his eyes, imagining the loss he'd felt the last several months without Jane. They just clicked. He'd finally found that best friend he wanted to kiss.

Man, he missed those lips. Soft, feminine … and so delightful.

He frowned as the kettle began to whistle. But what did he do wrong at the wedding? And where was he to go from here? What if Jane moved on? He headed toward the kitchen. Wait a minute. Was she dating someone new? Was that why she'd acted differently? His heart dropped before he remembered. No, they had been developing a killer online relationship. There was nothing wrong there. She'd been more than eager to start something new with him.

Shaking his head, he poured the water into the cocoa and stirred. Why were women so difficult, anyway? So lost in his thoughts, he burned his mouth as he sipped, then spilled a bit on the floor as he jerked the mug away. Ugh.

Suddenly, the doorbell rang.

"Just a second!"

Charles grumbled to himself as he wet a cloth and scooped up the mess. By the time he'd cleaned it up, his grandma was coming in through the door. He could barely make out her face over the large basket in her arms.

"Well, are you going to answer the door or not?" she asked.

He set his mug down, rushed forward, and collected the load from her. "What are you doing here? And what have you brought? You didn't carry this all the way from your car, did you?"

She rolled her eyes and bustled her way into his dining room. "Of course I did. Why do you young people always think we old folks can't do a dang thing for ourselves? It's ridiculous. When my dad was my age, he was still doing construction work!"

Great-grandpa had quit construction work at forty, but Charles didn't dare disagree.

"Bring it in here. It's your welcome present from your grammy."

"You didn't have to." Already, the smells coming from inside were making his mouth water. He couldn't resist a peek under the kitchen towel she had across the top. "No way. You made lemon bars too?"

Grammy grinned and winked. "Only if you're good." Then she made a fuss of clearing off his nearly pristine table. "Just set it down so you can open it." There was no doubt she was just as excited as he was.

"But it's not Christmas yet!" Charles chuckled at the frown on her face as he set it down where she directed.

"Stop teasing. And hurry up. Some of those things won't last two days before Christmas. Besides, I figured you wouldn't have a lick to eat, so I was sure to bring all your favorites."

He took off the towel and then grinned like a fool.

She didn't even waste time letting him decide what to pull out. "Okay. So I've got you your favorite chili, and I

17

made you some stew." She set them on the table. "And I've got your lemon bars, some muffins, and my rolls that you like so much. Grandpa gotcha some meat and cheese in here somewhere for those rolls. And I've got some gravy mixed up in this here Tupperware, and some biscuit mix for you to make your own biscuits one of these mornings. You're gonna need to put some of this in the fridge. I've got some grape juice and tomato juice that I've canned. And some of your favorite whole wheat bread with the honey butter. Oh! And Grandpa made you a whole bag of candy popcorn balls!"

"Wow!" It really was the best gift she could've ever given him. And there was no way he could properly repay this adorable burst of energy in his kitchen. So he leaned down and gave her a big hug and kissed those rosy cheeks. "Thank you, Grammy. You're the best!"

She chuckled and pushed him away, but that smile did wonders for his soul. "I'm just happy you're back for a while." Waggling her brows, she leaned in closer. "So, is it true? You gonna finally win over the other Bennet girl?"

There were no secrets ever in his family. Ever. Charles buried a sigh. "Can I get you some herbal tea or hot chocolate?"

"Will you tell me your plans?" Her eyes were twinkling.

All at once, he wondered if his mother and sisters had set Grammy up to pry information out of him. He was about to say no, but then again, maybe she could help. "Actually, I was hoping to talk to you about that."

"Really?"

He could've sworn he heard a muffled giggle come out of her.

"I'll take whatever herbal tea you've got. Let's sit in the living room, and you can tell me all about it."

Charles shook his head at her giddiness and pulled out the old tea box his mom had given him years ago. He never drank tea, but he always felt guilty for wanting to throw it away, so there it sat in his cupboard, waiting for gossipy old women to come along. "Raspberry?"

"Perfect. I'll wait in the other room."

He smiled wryly as he poured some hot water into the other mug and then joined her on the couch with his still-warm cocoa. They chatted for a bit about this and that, and then she nailed him.

"So, Chazz, tell me what's up. What would you like to know?"

Chazz. He grinned. No one had called him that for a long time. He took a deep breath and then sipped his cocoa without scalding himself this time. "Jane seemed off tonight. After I left you guys, I went to talk to her and say hi."

She nodded and took a sip of her drink, but didn't say anything.

"And . . . I don't know . . . Jane seemed different. Well, at first she seemed excited to see me—she even kissed me! But then that changed, and she got all stiff and just walked away. Right when I'd been hoping to really talk and apologize, she just left—said she was busy or something. It was weird."

Grammy looked at him and then asked, "Did she say anything? Ask how you were, you know, anything like that? Or did she just walk up and kiss you?"

He shrugged. "She asked normal things, like how long had I been there. And I explained why I hadn't sat next to her during dinner."

She fidgeted and nearly spilled her tea. "You were her dinner partner?"

"Um, yeah. Why are you looking at me like that?"

"You left her alone the whole time, and didn't say hi until during the toasts? She didn't know you had arrived yet?"

"Well, no. Is that a big deal or something?"

"Charles Fredrick Bingley! You are as absolutely clueless as your grandfather!"

"So her attitude is my fault? What did I do wrong?"

Grammy placed her mug on the coffee table in front of them and then put her hands dramatically on her face. "You need some help. You need some *real* help. Thank the good Lord I came today because this relationship would've been over before it had a chance."

He was way out of his depth here. "What?"

She leaned over and patted his knee. "What have you gotten her for Christmas?"

"Uh, a New York snow globe and warm blanket. Why? Is that bad too?"

She shook her head in a disbelieving manner. "Toss them both out. We're starting from scratch."

From scratch? "What do you have in mind?"

"Christmas. All twelve days of them."

"Twelve days?" What in the world was she talking about?

"Yes! And this time you're going to do things right!"

CHAPTER THREE

A Partridge in a Pear Tree

Jane got up from the couch and then sat down upon the matching striped gray chair in her apartment's living room. She sighed and crossed her legs. A few moments later, she unfolded them and stood up again.

Christmas Day. It had been two days since the wedding. Two. And she still hadn't heard from Charles. Her heart was too agitated to focus on anything. She was antsy. She was bored. She was nervous and frustrated and anxiety-ridden.

She should probably go shopping or something, but it was Christmas, and everything was closed. Pacing on her small white-and-turquoise rug, she debated what to do. She'd already been to her parents' house for Christmas gifts. She was supposed to stay longer, but honestly couldn't bear the happy chatter another moment, so she feigned a headache and went home. Now would've been the perfect time to call Eliza and moan, but no way was she going to interrupt her sister on her honeymoon. In fact, she doubted she'd ever be able to really interrupt her again.

Jane walked into the bedroom and picked up a book before setting it back down again. No. There was no way she could concentrate well enough to read, either. She saw her coat flung on the bed. A walk. Maybe that would work. She tossed it over her shoulders and grabbed a bright red-and-white striped scarf. She had to do something. Anything to take her mind off the fact that Charles was in town and they were supposed to spend the holidays together, and now it looked like she might have blown it.

Not that she should care. No girl deserves that kind of anxiety. But really, was he going to stop by or not? Why hadn't he texted or anything since she left him standing there? She took a deep breath, wrapped the scarf around her neck, and headed out the door.

She almost slipped on the ice, she was moving so fast, but her hand caught the railing just as her boots started to skid. Taking it a bit slower, she headed down the steps of the two-story building to the parking lot and then turned toward the park. The complex was only a couple of years old, and in a nice part of town.

Jane waved to a few neighbors as they were making their way into the complex. She would have jogged slightly to avoid having to make small talk, but the ground was icy. Instead, she kept her head lowered and walked the two hundred yards or so to the snow-filled park. There was a path that still hadn't been shoveled because of the holiday, with only a few smatterings of footprints and paw prints. She trudged through the soft fluff.

After about thirty minutes of breathing in clean, quiet air, she felt her mind might be settled enough to head back in. That, and her toes were beginning to go numb.

As she stomped her way back up the apartment stairs—attempting to get as much snow off as possible—she failed to notice the lone figure waiting at her door until she almost ran into him.

"Hi." Charles grinned and took a step toward her.

One word, and her heart calmed and her breathing went back to normal. He came. "Merry Christmas." Why did she feel like crying all of a sudden? She had no idea how much she'd missed that smile until she worried she'd never see it again.

"Merry Christmas to you too." He pointed down. "I brought you something."

There by his feet stood a miniature tree. "A plant?"

He bent down and picked it up. "Not just any plant. It's a pear tree. And it's also the reason I'm late. Apparently not many greenhouses around here carry pear trees this far into the season."

Charles went looking specifically for a pear tree? "Aren't the greenhouses all closed this time of year?"

He nodded. "Pretty much."

She didn't know quite what to say. "Well, thank you. It's . . . it's fun." Who wouldn't want their own miniature pear tree in December? The important thing was that he was here and trying. And sort of totally adorable.

His grin grew. "Do you really like it? I had to go to Vegas to get it, and I wasn't sure what your reaction would be. Because, you know, it's a fruit tree for Christmas. Well, for part of your Christmas. You're going to get a few more things from me."

"I am?" She chuckled. "Well, come on in, and you can tell me all about it. Though, I don't have a ton of stuff for you."

She held the door open for him as he scooped up another wrapped parcel and then followed her in.

"Ahh, it's so warm in here!"

"I would hope so." Jane chuckled as she gathered up a few holiday cards on a small table near the window. "You can set the tree here." After he put it down, she caught a glimpse of his red nose. "Oh, no. How long were you out there waiting for me? You look frozen."

"Um, not too long. Maybe twenty minutes or so."

After she turned up the gas fireplace, took his coat, and started cocoa on the stove, they sat down together on the couch, and he placed the second gift on her lap.

"There. Open it now, or the pear tree will never make sense."

She gave him a funny look, but was too curious to protest. "Okay, but after I do, you have to open yours." Tugging at the taped edges of the gold wrapping paper, she pulled out the small blue box and gently took off the top. There, nestled amongst soft white tissue paper, was the prettiest silver bird ornament. "It's so beautiful." But she had no clue how the two gifts correlated at all. She held the delicate ornament up and watched as the bird gracefully spun from its cord wrapped around her finger. In her confusion, she glanced over at Charles. "What does it mean?"

One eyebrow rose, and his handsome grin peeked out. "It's a partridge."

As if that was helpf—"Oh! Like the song."

He nodded. "On the first day of Christmas…"

She chimed in, her heart beginning to skip, "My true love gave to me…"

"A partridge in a pear tree."

He took the ornament from her, leaned over to the tree, and slipped the cord onto a branch. "There. The first day of Christmas."

Jane rolled her eyes. "But it's not the first day of Christmas—it's the last."

"You're wrong. In the olden days, this is how England celebrated Christmas."

She gave him a funny look and glanced back at the tree. "Are you serious? The twelve days of Christmas actually started on Christmas Day?"

"Yep." He looked mighty smug, and then moved a bit closer. "The first day of Christmas was actually the twenty-fifth or twenty-sixth, depending on your family traditions. Then on Boxing Day, they would box up or wrap up all of the gifts to take around to their neighbors and family beginning the second day of Christmas. Some homes had a gift or celebration for every day of Christmas running all the way until January fifth—or sixth—and on Twelfth Night, they'd have a big feast."

"I had no idea. But I don't understand. Why would you go to all the trouble?"

"Because I should. Because you're worth it. To make up for all the days I've missed." He clasped his hands together and took a deep breath, then glanced up at her. "The thing is, I realized I screwed up the other day—actually, long before that. I sort of ruined us before we really had a chance to begin. And I know how much you love Jane Austen and that simpler lifestyle, and I don't know—I thought I'd be the first man to give you a real traditional Christmas."

My true love? The words of the carol rang through her mind, but she didn't have the guts to say them out loud. "So, are you saying you're going to give me gifts each day until January, or something?"

"Not just any gift!" He sat up straighter. "But the words of the song. I've decided that if you're ever going to believe me and see that I'm serious about us, I'd better do things right. Besides, who wouldn't want to spread this amazing holiday out just a little bit longer?"

"But I only have one present for you."

"Then save it until Twelfth Night." He smiled as if that would make everything all right.

CHAPTER FOUR

Two Turtle Doves

Charles whistled the whole drive home that night. Jane had successfully—after many failed attempts—gotten it out of him that all of this was Grammy's idea, but he didn't care. The stunned look on her face was worth every second of the surprise. Every. Darn. Freezing. Second it took waiting for her to come home.

He took a deep breath as he pulled into his driveway. Man, he loved that woman. Everything about her warmed him. She fit so well, he couldn't believe he'd allowed himself to go this long without mending their relationship. Now to get her to trust him and forgive him for breaking her heart … and hopefully, just hopefully, they'd have perfection again.

* * *

He had arranged to meet up with Jane at eleven the next morning. Since she was off work until the fourth of January—thank goodness for school holiday breaks!—it gave him a complete advantage. They could make their plans at any time during the day, and he basically had her all to himself. This time, as he walked into her door, he carried a large Christmas bag with tissue paper and a bow on it.

"What's that?" Jane chuckled. "Please don't tell me you have two poor doves in that bag. Please."

Charles walked all the way into her kitchen and set the gift down on her table. "And who wouldn't love two turtle doves?"

"Uh, me." She grinned and accepted the hug he gave her. "How are you doing today?"

"Well, I was good until you completely broke my heart. I can't believe you've already rejected my gift before you've even opened it." He unzipped his coat and hung it on the chair nearest him.

"I never said I rejected it. Just that I didn't want two turtle doves." She turned and pulled some sandwiches and potato salad from the fridge. "Hungry?"

His mouth began to water. "Starving. How can I help?" Before she could answer, he walked over to the cupboard and pulled out two small plates, and then went in search of some silverware. "How is it that I remembered where your plates are, but can't remember which of these drawers holds the forks?"

She set the food down on the table—its bright red tablecloth contrasted nicely with the delicious-looking lunch. "Left one, next to the sink."

"Ah! Got it." He grinned and walked over to her with the silverware. "Next you're going to be complaining that you don't want French hens or laying geese, aren't you?"

Jane scooted past him and grabbed a couple of white napkins from a basket on the counter, and then collected a spatula. "Don't forget about eight maids a-milking. What in the world would I do with them? This place isn't big enough—or for all that milk, either!"

He put his hands in the air as he sat down. "See? You've completely thrown off my whole groove now. How am I supposed to re-create this amazingly thoughtful Christmas for you if you keep seeing it in such a negative light?"

Jane's eyes sparkled as she attempted not to laugh. "I'm sure you'll try to convince me that the twelve drummers drumming were meant to be a good idea as well."

"You know me. I think we should invite them to the wedding. They could perform an awesome drumline. Think of it—all lined up in kilts."

"Kilts?" She sat down and began to pass out the sandwiches. "What kilts? And more importantly, what wedding again?"

He pulled his chair next to hers and held up his plate as she placed an extra-large sandwich on it. "Ours, of course." There—he had to say it just to watch her reaction. Jane didn't disappoint. She nearly dropped the sandwich she was holding. She might have thought he didn't notice, but he did.

"Ours?" She laughed a little too forcefully. "I don't remember ever agreeing to marry you. Don't we have to backtrack a little?'

"Nah." He smiled as he took a bite of bliss. Tuna salad. Man, it was good. After he swallowed, he added, "I figured after all the gifts and crazy amount of people I'd have to coerce into performing them for you, you'd have to marry me." He took another bite and moaned. "This is so good. Thank you."

"I'm glad you like it." She put a scoop of potato salad on his plate too.

After he dug into the potato salad, his mouth was in heaven. "I'm glad you like to cook." He took two more bites and then pushed the gift toward her. "In fact, that reminds me."

"The doves?" She set her fork down. "You want me to open the doves now?"

"Of course."

"But can't I at least finish lunch before they flit about everywhere?"

"Where's the fun in that? Who doesn't love flitting turtle doves?"

She chuckled. "I have no idea."

"Are you going to open it or not?"

"Yes." She gave him a playful look. "Are you always this impatient?"

Was she serious? "Only when I'm desperate to please the most amazing woman on earth. Yes, okay. I'm impatient. I'm excited for you to see what I got. Now put me out of my misery and open the darn thing."

She bit her lip and leaned back in her chair. Her lashes kissed her cheeks for a brief moment before startling blues eyes met his. How could he think for one moment that this woman wasn't perfect for him? He was more than head over heels… he was borderline smitten.

Jane had such a calming way about her. Those tumultuous eyes were the only sign that her brain was going a million miles a minute. Her demeanor was so poised and collected—elegant. The word he was looking for was elegant. The woman had more class in her sweet grin than most women could ever hope to possess in their whole lives.

That serene poise was what first drew him to her during the holiday office party. She was so mysterious and quietly mature, she put all the overly bright, gossipy women to shame. As much as he was impatient when he was excited—so he liked to complete his goals. Sue him—he was also very much an old soul. His fast-paced work life craved peace. Someone to quiet his mind and settle his harried thoughts and bring harmony. He longed for someone to laugh with—not to mock others, but to find joy in the simple things of life. Someone to read with, to ponder life's mysteries, and someone to enjoy a debate, without clashing, but to appreciate the differences between them.

Jane was that woman—and so much more. She was quick, but never quick to judge or speak. She took her time to explore a thought, and rarely jumped to rash conclusions. Everything came in stride. In many ways, those few short months with her proved to be some of the most memorable teaching moments he'd ever known. She'd quietly bring his own fears down and talk sense into him, showing him that the world had more than one reality. There was always another way, another hope, another light to be lit.

Slowly, Jane pulled the gift toward her and then revealed why she had put off opening it. "I really don't understand why you feel the need to buy me so many gifts. I didn't get you much—which you still haven't opened—" She pointed to the room where he'd left the parcel the night before. "And now I feel bad opening yet another present from you."

He shook his head. "Please don't. We agreed to wait until the last day of Christmas, remember?"

"You agreed. I didn't say anything."

Was this really going to be a problem? "Would you like me to open it now?"

She winced. "No. Yes. I don't know. I just wish we could celebrate this together, and without you opening gifts too, I don't think it's fair."

Was that all? He laughed and gestured toward the bag. "Open it. You'll see."

Finally, her curiosity won out, and she removed the tissue paper and peeked inside. "What?" He grinned as she pulled out first one bag of Dove chocolates, and then another. Soon, a bag of caramels and a bag of pecans joined them. "What is this?"

"Two turtle doves, of course."

It took her a moment, puzzling over the four bags before her face lit up. "We're making chocolate turtles out of Dove chocolate."

"Yep."

"Together. As in, this was what you had planned for today?" Her grin was contagious.

"Unless you can think of something else…"

"No! I love it. This is perfect. And we can share." She stood up and got two aprons, tossing one to him. "Put this on and start unwrapping those caramels! We need some dessert to go with that lunch."

"Bossy." What was it about confident women that caused his heart to flip?

They spent the next thirty minutes or so making a much bigger mess in the kitchen than either wanted to admit. "That chocolate on the cupboard doors has to be from you. My bowl is still perfect, see?"

Jane laughed and flung a chunk of chocolate from her bowl to his. "There. Now it's messy too."

Charles gasped and then saved the random chunk by eating it. They were going to create two huge chocolate turtles, but after several attempts, decided that a bunch of smaller ones would be much better.

They were. The whole day was as perfect as it could be. After they ate way too much chocolate, and then cleaned up their mess, Charles and Jane sat down in the small living room and talked and laughed and slowly began to dream again. His heart nearly tripled as she stood up on tiptoe and kissed him as he left.

"What time tomorrow?" she asked, her voice a bit deeper than usual.

"What's tomorrow? The third day? Oh! That's a fun one. You do have an evening gown, right?"

Her eyebrows rose. "An evening gown? Are you kidding? For what?"

"To get your French hens, of course."

CHAPTER FIVE

Three French Hens

Jane shook her head as she closed the door on that exasperatingly smug grin. Charles was enjoying this all too much. As she walked into the kitchen, she found herself thinking about his easy-going manner that day. Eight months, and it was as if he'd never left—or even better than that. It was as if they'd been together all that time and had only grown stronger. Her heart skipped a bit when she saw his adorable attempt at making chocolate turtles. Ten points for trying. The man certainly was no Julia Child or Martha Stewart, but what he lacked in skill, he certainly made up for with his willingness and fun attitude.

She chuckled and then paused a moment. Just as soon as she had laughed, she began to cry. Without reason, those silly stupid tears began to fall. Turning off the lights, she made her way to her bedroom, curled up on her pretty white four-poster bed, and sobbed into her blue lace pillow.

She'd believed she'd never have this type of crazy fun again, but here he was. Her own foolish Christmas wish come true—the man she'd given up on was actually making an effort to see her again. This was real. And she had ten more marvelous days to enjoy it.

A part of her wondered if she'd wake up and find herself still on Christmas Day, anxiety-ridden and asleep on the couch, dreaming up this whole magical thing.

She wiped at her eyes and rolled over, staring at her ceiling. What if at the end of this, things fell apart again? Could she bear the separation, the rejection? What if this really was all just a fun, fleeting moment? What if he suddenly decided he didn't want her again? Jane took a moment and allowed that thought to wrap itself around her, its cold, sad vibe paralyzing her limbs. What if she really wasn't worth all the effort?

This was silly. She had to stay strong. Or learn to let go, and just accept that things will happen as they will. No one could control what would happen over the next week or so, but was she willing to push away the possibility of happiness because she was afraid of rejection again?

No.

Jane took a deep breath and closed her eyes. Her whole life consisted of thinking of others first, of hoping for the best. She refused to follow the latest gossip, or engage in petty arguments. People said she wore rose-colored glasses, and maybe she did. But why was it so hard to imagine that Charles could possibly be sincere? Why could she so easily believe that he would leave her again, when everything he was doing now should prove that he wanted her and wanted a future with her?

What if she wasn't worth it? What if she was never meant to hold her own against a rising star in the business world? What was she, after all, but an elementary school librarian? Nothing of importance. Just a girl who gave up her dreams to help her Aunt Phyllis. Not that she regretted it—of course not. To see the children's eyes flash once she got them hooked on reading was worth every lost opportunity with her chosen profession.

When she woke up the next morning, Jane rummaged through her closet and couldn't come up with anything remotely resembling an evening gown. The closest thing she could find was the dress she wore for Eliza's wedding, but it wasn't long enough. It only came to her knees. Besides, she wanted something splashy. Something pretty and elegant, but flattering, too.

After a few hurried texts where she confirmed Charles wouldn't be showing up until six that night, she grabbed her purse and her sister's extra key and headed over to Eliza's house. She was supposed to be watering the plants and bringing in the mail anyway. She'd bet a hundred dollars her sister had the perfect dress hanging unused in her closet.

Eliza really had to ramp up her wardrobe when she began working with Will. The two sisters had spent countless hours at the mall and online ordering outfits that could travel easily and still be stunning enough to go to cocktail parties and fancy dinners and upscale business meetings. After Eliza had chewed Will out over his lacking wardrobe, the two sisters knew she'd never hear the end of it if she didn't absolutely rock everything she wore.

As Jane pushed open the front door, there was only a slight feeling of unease. Just that little knowledge that you're all alone in a place. She set the mail on top of a pink notebook on the table nearest the couch and then quickly headed into the bedroom. There were a few boxes around, but no serious packing had been done yet. Eliza still had two months left on the lease, so she had planned to move into Will's holy-amazing mansion slowly.

Jane sifted through several dresses. It looked like Eliza had taken all of the really pretty ones for her honeymoon, which was totally understandable. Jane was about to go ahead and wear her silver one from the wedding after all, when she caught a faint glitter from the back. Hidden behind some jackets was a plastic-wrapped gown. It was a chic black color, and attached to the plastic was a note that read, "For Jane. Merry Christmas."

"What?" Jane blinked. "Are you kidding me?" Didn't they already exchange gifts? She thought of the pearl earrings and matching bracelet she'd given Eliza right before the wedding, but she couldn't recall what Eliza had given her. In all the frazzled preparations, did she forget?

Jane whisked the plastic off the dress and found a beautifully laced and beaded mermaid gown. It was floor length and gorgeous. Two pretty capped sleeves accented the top, though it was the gold, maroon, and white floral brooch that was pinned at the waist that really set off the gown. It was almost bridal in design, except in sophisticated black. Had Eliza known she would need this exact dress?

There was no way. Even Charles didn't realize he was planning the twelve days of Christmas until now. After holding the dress up and twirling around in front of the mirror, she headed home to try it on and get ready.

All day, she primped and pampered herself until she literally glowed when Charles knocked on the door.

"Wow! You look beautiful." His wide eyes and smile was all the compliment she needed.

"Wow yourself. A tux? You didn't even wear a tux to the wedding." What was it about a man in a well-tailored tux that could take your breath away?

"Don't you like it?"

"Definitely," she said, hoping she didn't sound too eager. Clearing her throat, she finished lamely, "It works on you."

He winked. "Glad to know you approve. So, are you ready to go?"

"Yes, but I still have no idea how French hens and dressing posh correlate."

"Oh, ye of little faith. You must trust me. Now where's your coat?"

It wasn't until he pulled onto the grounds of La Caille, one of the ritziest French restaurants in Utah, that she realized they might possibly be eating the French hens. She had never personally eaten there, but had heard how incredible the food was.

She grinned as he opened her car door, knowing he couldn't deny it now. "So you're taking me out for French chicken?"

"Only if you don't like my actual plan. But knowing your love of seafood, I'm going to assume that chicken will be the last thing you order."

What in the world was he on about? "Seafood?"

"Aha! The librarian doesn't know everything!" He tucked her hand into the crook of his elbow and walked her toward the beautifully decorated restaurant.

It looked like something straight from Europe. The grounds were elegant, and Jane jumped when a large, colorful bird flew in front of her up into one of the nearest trees. Its wings were bright blue, and feathers a distinct green against the white of the snow around them. "Was that a peacock?"

"Yes. Pretty, isn't it?"

"Peacocks live in Utah?"

"La Caille has had peafowl for years. I believe it may be the largest community of the birds in the state."

She glanced around the formal gardens and took in the big lake, ornamental bridges, cobblestone paths, and glowing fairy lights. "I bet this place looks breathtaking in the summer."

"Fantastic venue for a wedding."

Wedding. She caught her breath as she glanced into his dark eyes. "I don't think I've ever heard a man say something like that."

He blushed slightly and looked down, and then those eyes met hers again. "What? Can't a man think of planning weddings like you women do?"

She shrugged and began to walk toward the building, trying as best she could to keep calm—though her heart was definitely betraying her. "Never really thought about it before."

By the time they were seated in the elegant, lavishly decorated dining room, her heart had almost returned to normal. She glanced around the room and took note of the large chandeliers and Christmas greenery boughs. Their decorator deserved whatever praise they received. It was like stepping back in time to a magical place.

"Can I order for us both?" Charles was searching through the menu.

"Of course, but I'm not certain I should trust you."

He chuckled and glanced up at her. "I always knew you were an intelligent woman."

"So, what do you have in mind?"

"Three French hens, remember?"

She tried not to roll her eyes as she shook her head. "Yes, and you said we weren't eating chicken."

Just then, the waitress came over with their drinks. "Are you ready to order?"

One final glance at Jane before he ordered. "Yes. We'd like to start with an artisanal cheese board, and then lobster bisque, and halibut a la Basquaise. Oh, and please add a lobster tail to each dinner course as well."

Jane nearly choked. "Charles, that's a ton of food. How in the world will I ever eat it?"

He winked again. "If there are leftovers—which I doubt—you'll enjoy them too." He took a sip of his water. "Besides, I haven't even ordered the dessert. I thought you'd like to do that afterward."

"Thank you, sir. Any drinks?"

His eyes roamed over Jane, as if he wished they were alone. She wasn't even sure he heard. "Not yet. We'll let you know if we need something," she replied. He still hadn't stopped staring at her. Once the waitress left, she asked, "What?"

His eyes softened, and he shook his head slightly. Everything in the room seemed to freeze at once. Even her breathing became much more pronounced.

"I don't know," he said quietly. "It just hit me, I'm actually here at La Caille with the most beautiful woman in the world—and I began to wonder how such a thoughtless person could be as lucky as I am."

She looked down as she felt her neck and cheeks redden, having no idea how to respond to him. Where to start? "You're not thoughtless, and I certainly wouldn't say I was the most be—"

"Beautiful person in the world? You only say that because you can't see how you sparkle compared to everyone else. You honestly can't see yourself."

If he didn't stop, she'd turn as red as the lobster tails he'd ordered.

"And you're wrong." He leaned forward. "I am thoughtless. I'm completely stupid. And I ask myself constantly how you could forgive me as well as you have."

Here it was. That confession she knew he'd give. She dreaded hearing why everything stopped, his real reason for leaving—reminding her that at any time, he could decide she wasn't enough again. Her heart clenched, and one hand braced against the linen tablecloth. Her mouth dropped open slightly, but she couldn't say anything. She had no words.

It didn't matter. Charles wasn't done by a long shot. "I need to apologize for ending this—us—and taking off to New York, and basically leaving you hanging with the lamest excuse of not wanting to try a long-distance relationship."

"Charles—"

He shook his head. "No, I need to get this out there. Just a minute and then we can talk, but first, please let me genuinely apologize for my mistake. I could blame several different things, but honestly, I was scared. The error is mine, and I own it. If I'd listened to my heart, this never would've happened. Had I been man enough to accept how I really feel, I'm certain you and I would be having a very different conversation over this dinner."

He reached over and tenderly held her hand.

"Jane, I love you. I know that now. I wasn't sure before, but without you, I'm completely miserable. I can see in your eyes that you doubt me, but I will prove it to you. And if one day down the road, you're able to see past my faults and still find that spark we once had, then I'll celebrate." He took a deep breath. "However, no pressure. If all we ever become is friends, I'll be forever grateful for whatever time I get to spend with you."

Her mind was whirling with a thousand questions—what did he mean, if he had listened to his heart? Was there something more to the story? But her questions were drowned out by the frantic beating of her heart.

"And Jane, forgive me for the way I acted at your sister's wedding. Honestly, I was frightened. I knew I didn't deserve you. And when I first saw you, leaning over whispering something to Eliza and then laughing, I started to shake. I'm not kidding—my knees actually began to tremble. I had no idea the effect you had on me until that moment, and I needed time to compose myself. What I didn't realize was that I'd taken too much time and had hurt you again before I'd even had a chance to make up for the past.

"I'm stumbling over my words. I don't think men in general were meant to actually communicate with women." He grinned. "No, I'm serious. I think we mess up so much that God probably intended for us to be mute just so we wouldn't be so impolite. Except Eve probably begged for Adam to have a voice, thinking she honestly wanted his opinion, and ruined it completely for the rest of you."

She raised an eyebrow. "So, are you implying Eve is to blame for the ridiculous things men say?"

He leaned back and put his hands up in front of him. "See what I mean? We aren't supposed to talk."

Jane chuckled as the waitress walked over with their bread and cheese. "You certainly do keep things exciting. And what girl doesn't love a little drama?"

After the dinner course was over and she'd eaten all she could, and they were making their way back home, Jane couldn't help but ask, "So, where are the French hens?"

Charles pulled his phone from his jacket pocket and handed it to her. "Google the word 'hen.'"

Jane didn't even have to Google. She looked up, shocked she hadn't thought of it before. "Female lobsters are hens!"

He grinned. "La Caille lobster bisque, lobster tails—I'm sure we've had our fair share of French hens today."

"You got me on that one. I can't believe I didn't think of how to correlate the two."

He glanced over and waggled his brows in the darkness of the car. "Just wait until tomorrow."

"Four calling birds, right?" She leaned back in her seat and sighed happily. Who would have thought this Christmas would be so fun? "And how would you like me to dress?"

"Warm. There's snow on the ground, and we're going to be taking a stroll."

"So, warm as in, jacket and gloves? Or should I put on my snow boots and coat?"

"Definitely the snow boots. I'll be here at noon," he said as he pulled up into her complex. Then he leaned over and kissed her, his soft lips mingling perfectly with hers.

CHAPTER SIX

Four Calling Birds

Charles approached Jane's house and took the steps two at a time. When he almost slipped on the last one, he decided to slow things down a bit as he approached her door. Gotta love looking like a dork as you get ready to take a hot girl out on a date. There were some days he felt like he was eighteen again, all sweaty palms and bumbling feet.

When she opened the door with that sweet smile, his world collapsed around him. "Hello," he said, not sure if he was capable of saying another word.

"Hi."

She looked charming in a blue-and-white coat, white pants and snow boots, and a matching blue scarf and hat. Part of him wanted to call the whole thing off and stay indoors, sipping hot cocoa and staring into those pretty eyes of hers. Who was he kidding? He was dying to taste those lips again too.

But slowly. He had to work slow and casually, or he'd never convince her he was sincere. Isn't that what Grammy was always saying? "Treat a girl like she's worth the wait, and you'll keep her forever." Jane Bennet was so worth the wait.

"Have you eaten yet?" he asked her.

"Um, yes, a little." She bit her lip. "I wasn't sure what we were doing."

"We're going back to La Caille, so I hope you've got some room left."

He loved the confused look on her face. Honestly, why were they going anywhere? Why wasn't he proposing this second and sweeping her off to Vegas and then on a romantic honeymoon?

"Why La Caille again? I mean, don't get me wrong—it was so wonderful—but you told me to dress like this, and I . . ."

He grinned and pulled her out of the doorway. "It's fine. We're not going in the restaurant this time. Now, lock up and let's go before I change my mind and decide to snuggle with you on the couch instead."

"But . . ." She pouted as she slipped the key in place, locking the door. "What if I want to snuggle all day on the couch?"

His heart skipped a beat and then jolted to a stop. There was nothing, nothing he'd like to do more. "But you wouldn't get your present for the day."

"Fine. Then let's hurry this time because I'd love to be held by you and just talk tonight."

He took a deep breath, attempting to calm his rising heart rate. "You win. First, on to four calling birds."

Ryan, the groundskeeper, greeted them as they pulled onto the restaurant grounds. Charles had arranged for him to give them a tour. Jane might have thought the restaurant itself was beautiful, but he couldn't wait to show her the whole property. La Caille had something like twenty-four acres spread out to call home. And this time, he was taking her to see all of the peacocks. No one knew the birds better than Ryan did, and Charles couldn't wait to surprise her with how cool La Caille really was.

As they toured the property, even Charles was impressed with all they had going on. Ryan showed them the delightful hidden-away cottages for rent and the winding paths, perfect for romantic rendezvous or for photos. Apart from the large lake on the property, there was also a vineyard, garden, gazebo, and of course elegant bridges, streams, and ponds. But it was the peacocks that really fascinated Jane—just like he knew they would.

One particularly large Indian Blue peacock followed them for some time. His cheerful call was exactly what Charles hoped it would be.

Jane caught on immediately. "Oh, so you're my calling bird!" She grinned and reached out to pet him—they were on the cobblestone path leading back from one of the cottages. He called again, but didn't move. Tilting his head, he blinked at Jane and waited.

"He wants you to feed him," Ryan said as he fished something out of his pocket. "Here. Take these dried peaches."

"Thank you." Jane was all smiles as she approached the bird with her offering. "Here you go, sir." She glanced back at us. "What's his name? Does he have one?"

Ryan nodded. "Not all of the birds do, but this is Taj Mahal. He's about three or four years old, but he's been this friendly since he was a baby. One of our frequent guests named him, and it sort of stuck."

"I love it. It's the perfect name." The bird called again, and then leaned in and quickly snatched a piece of dried peach from Jane's hand. Soon, other peafowl were swooping in and landing around them. White, green, blue—so many beautiful colors! Charles didn't think he'd ever seen Jane so enchanted before.

"Oh wow! This is amazing!" she gasped as she glanced around at the fifteen or so birds.

They called and chirped at her, and she broke apart the peaches to make sure everyone got one.

There was something so graceful about them. "They're rather tame. Is it because they've always lived here?" Charles asked.

Ryan nodded. "That, and peafowl are very peaceful birds. They believe in harmony, more than, say, a rooster or turkey—they don't battle that much. Instead, they prance around, showing off their feathers." He pointed to Taj Mahal. "What you see now is nothing. By this summer, his tail will be in long and full again. Every fall, they lose their tail feathers, but come mating season, they grow back."

"I believe they might be the most beautiful birds I've ever seen." Jane crouched down as a smaller bird cooed its way over to her legs, begging for more treats. She was able to pet his soft feathers before he scattered back a few feet. "I would love to have some of my own."

"They make incredible pets. Most of these birds will live thirty years easily, if they're well fed and cared for."

"Really?" She giggled as a larger green peacock pushed his way through the others to coo right up at her. "I've never seen such friendly birds before, and I would've never guessed they'd still be out and about in all the snow."

Charles's heart warmed as he watched the way her whole face lit up around the birds. Her wonder made him wish he'd known her when she was a child.

Ryan shrugged. "They love the snow, and will still roost in the trees at night as long as it's clear out. During storms, you'll find them huddled together in some of the shelters we have around here, but mostly, they do just fine in these temperatures."

"My, aren't you greedy?" She laughed as the larger male continued to nudge her hand with his head, his top feathers waving frantically as he did so. Jane looked up with her joyful grin, her eyes connecting with Charles's. "Aren't they amazing? I think I'm in love."

Right then, Charles knew he had to surprise her with her own birds. He didn't know how yet, or when, but he vowed that Jane Bennet would have peafowl of her own one day.

CHAPTER SEVEN

Five Golden Rings

The next morning, Charles rang Jane's doorbell. It was still dark outside. Perfect. He'd always wondered what she looked like first thing in the morning.

"Who is it?" she asked through the door. Her groggy voice made him smile.

Someone was definitely enjoying her holiday without having to get up early for school.

"Me."

"Ugh. Are you serious?" She groaned as she opened the door. "When you said you'd be here in the morning, I actually thought you'd wait until the sun rose first." Yawning, she clutched her robe and stepped back into the apartment.

"Are you saying you don't like surprises?" he asked as he stepped over the threshold. He was careful not to tilt the package he held.

She flipped on a light and then squinted adorably at him. Her hair was every which way, which only caused him to smile more.

"I've never known a woman to be so grumpy about getting gifts."

"Yeah, well, this is a little excessive." She pushed her hair off her face and attempted a sad chuckle. "Admit it. You just wanted to come here so early to laugh at me."

He was about to answer, but her eyes must've cleared enough to see him because she groaned again. "Are you kidding me? Who looks as good as you do this early in the morning? It should be outlawed."

"Well, my dear, very few women have ever seen me this early in the morning. Consider it an incredible compliment." He pointed to the table. "Now, sit down so I can give you your five golden rings."

"What?" She walked over and sat. "This couldn't wait until later?"

"Ungrateful wretch."

She pouted. "I so am. But seriously, what did you expect?"

"Exactly this." He leaned over and kissed her pout and then pulled out the box he'd been carrying in his bag.

"Donuts?" she asked as he set it on the table.

"Yep. Golden, deliciously glazed donuts. See, they're rings." He smiled.

"Holy cow, they smell amazing."

"Nah, that's the hot cocoa." He pulled two large travel mugs from the bag too.

She dug into the box and melted as she took her first bite of donut. "You're a saint. A woke-me-up-too-early saint, but a saint nonetheless."

"Sure you don't mean monster? I mean, I wouldn't want this all to go to my head here."

"I would laugh, but this is too good. I could seriously eat this whole box. I suggest you don't watch."

"Hey! I think not." He reached over and snatched a donut for himself. "Remind me next time to go for an even dozen."

"I thought this was *my* gift."

"Touché." He nodded as he took a bite of his. "Remind me never to argue with you."

She took a sip of her cocoa. "Mmm… Yeah, it's pretty fruitless to attempt to argue with a woman." Setting her elbows on the table, she leaned forward. "Besides, it was probably your grammy and mom, anyway."

What in the . . . ? How could women flip conversations so easily? "What was?"

"The other women who've seen you this early in the morning." She grinned and took another bite.

To his great mortification, he could feel his cheeks going warm. "I refuse to answer that question."

She giggled. "You don't have to. I can see it on your face."

He was about to protest when she added, "And I love it!"

Charles knew when he'd been beaten, and he'd also learned a long time ago—from his grandpa, actually—when it was best to keep his mouth shut. This was definitely one of those times. Instead, he leaned over too and watched those mischievous eyes of hers dance about before he smirked and took a swig of his own cocoa. Nothing was better than silence and cocoa. Nothing. Except maybe being in the presence of a pretty girl at the same time.

The rest of the day was spent exploring and laughing and learning about each other, something that had been a long time coming. They discussed everything from books to television shows to favorite cars and dream holiday destinations.

"I've always dreamed of traveling to London!" she gasped. "Are you kidding me? You've been twice?" She scrambled and knelt on the couch, where they'd been sitting for nearly an hour. All at once, she was as giddy as a thirteen-year-old. "What was your favorite place? Did you do a lot of touring? What were you there for?" Jane tugged on his shirtsleeve. "Come on, I'm dying to know everything."

Fascinated by this new side of her, he was a bit stunned. He liked her this way—there was something so real, so unexpectedly free and sweet. "I was there for business meetings both times, so I didn't have a lot of time to explore. However, I did take one of those double-decker buses and did a quick tour around London that way."

"Was the city as beautiful as everyone says it is?"

He shook his head. "It's even more amazing than anything you've heard—more beautiful than anything you could possibly imagine. I think it's one of the most gorgeous cities in the world. Very well kept, not a lot of garbage, and stunning architecture everywhere. Some of the most incredible examples of the time periods around. The British certainly take care of their history."

"Oh, stop! I'm so jealous right now!" She leaned against the back of the couch and grinned. "Tell me more. I want to imagine every bit of it."

"I'll answer any questions you have. But first, haven't you wanted to explore other places too?"

Jane bit her lip and glanced around the room, and then leaned in and whispered. "You. Have. No. Idea."

"Why are we whispering?" he whispered back while stifling another chuckle.

"Because no one knows this about me. And I mean no one. Not even Eliza knows how badly I want to travel." She sighed. "And I will one day. I mean it. I'll see everywhere—Russia and China and Japan and Australia— Oh! And New Zealand too! And Ireland and Scotland, and of course England, but Turkey, Austria, Iceland, Spain, Italy…"

The first thing he would do once they were married was get her a passport. Every break they had, he'd whisk her away on a new adventure. He'd never felt such a need to do so much for someone else, but he'd be hung if he didn't give her this dream of hers. And he couldn't wait to see the joy on her face as she saw the world for the first time, as they traveled it together.

As he pulled into his driveway, the reality that his world would never be the same after that day hit home strong and hard. Honestly, if he didn't manage to win her hand after all this, he didn't know what he'd do.

CHAPTER EIGHT

Six Geese-a-Laying

Jane grinned in her bed as she closed her eyes, reliving the day she'd just had. Was this really happening? He was just wonderfully chill and fun and easygoing. And perfect. Dang it. Why did he have to be so perfect?

When she woke up, that deliciously warm feeling that stretched from her head to her toes was still there. Lightness. Giddiness. Everything. It was all there. And she couldn't wait to see what that day would bring.

She'd promised to take care of Eliza's place and water the plants—something she'd completely forgotten about when she was there a few days ago—so they agreed to meet up in the afternoon. Though to be honest, she easily could have had him over sooner. Like, right now. Why did she wave him off when he offered to run errands with her?

But how was she to know she'd spend the whole night dreaming about him and then the whole morning missing him? Sure, he said he was in love with her, but she'd been there before, so her heart wasn't as willing and trusting as it could have been. And it's better to be cautious, right?

She missed him. And the more they were together and talked, the more she could see this crazy future with him. He was making her dream of a life with him again, but this time, it was better somehow. This time, they were uncovering even more about each other than before.

She wished she could call Eliza up and tell her everything. Jane needed some girl time, but she wouldn't call. No matter how exhilarating her life was becoming, she wasn't willing to interrupt the newlyweds.

As she grabbed her purse and drove out of the complex, her cell phone rang. Her heart began to beat excitedly. Was it Eliza? Or better yet, Charles? It took a couple of tries to answer the phone, but it was her mom.

"Hey, what's up?" she asked as she pushed the disappointment away.

Her mom laughed. "You sound like you're happy. Do you have any news?"

Jane grinned and ruefully shook her head. Her mother could fish out the most hidden secrets from anyone. And the woman was completely good at reading a situation and knowing when something fabulous was going on. It was a gift Jane certainly didn't have. "What do you mean?" The last thing she needed was her mom to find out about Charles. She'd never hear the end of it.

"What do I mean? I mean, you sound happy. Now stop being silly and tell me."

"I'm just enjoying my break from school."

"Mm-hmm ... Your break from school that you're spending with Charles Bingley, right?"

Jane almost swerved the car. "How do you do it?"

"Do what, dear? Know when my daughters are about to get married?" She laughed. "Call it mother's intuition.

And also, it helps that Marianne down the street came over to tell me she saw you and Charles at La Caille the other night, and wants to know if you're back on again."

"And how does Marianne even know Charles and I were dating in the first place? As a matter of fact, how does she even know what Charles looks like?" What in the world?

"Hush. She doesn't. She just described him to me, and since I saw you two sneak off one after the other at the wedding, I sort of put things together."

"Are you kidding me? That doesn't even make sense." Her mother was also the master of half-truths and exaggerations. This conversation was not going well.

"No, I'm not kidding. Now, I've been recovering from all the wedding drama before Christmas, and I've been completely neglecting my motherly duties. So, I'm back. Thanks to Marianne. And anyway, Dad and I would like you guys to come over tomorrow for dinner. We're anxious to get to know Charles again."

Jane could've died. "Mom, no. What you mean is, you're anxious to start grilling Charles, and I'm not going to let that happen."

"Why not? He's a big boy. Besides, if you two are going to get married—and trust me, if the man is taking you to La Caille, things are getting serious—anyway, if he becomes a member of the family, then he needs to spend time with us and get to know us. You know, so he's comfortable."

"I don't know, Mom. I think this may be a little too soon."

"What? You want to keep him, don't you? This isn't too soon at all. You're forgetting how awesome we are, or you wouldn't be saying this. We throw fun dinner parties, remember?"

Jane took a deep breath. "I remember." She also remembered how many guys she'd dated who didn't have that much fun meeting her family. There were days when she wished she could actually say no, but then, she'd hurt her mom's feelings, so she didn't … but there were days.

And Mom was in full guilt-trip force. "I'll make lasagna. Your favorite."

The last thing Jane wanted was for the family to sit around eating lasagna while asking Charles thousands of questions, but she also knew her mother. If she didn't agree to something like this, before she knew it, Mom would start stalking them again. And heaven knew, a controlled environment was much better than surprise visits from Mom everywhere. "Fine. I'll talk to him and see what he says."

"Perfect!" She giggled. "I'll see you at five tomorrow."

"Five?" How long was this dinner party, anyway? "Five's a little early."

"No it's not! It's fine. Besides, your dad likes to go to bed a bit earlier lately."

"Sure. Blame Dad when we both know this is about you getting to know Charles. But wait until I talk to him! He might already have plans. I'll call you and confirm tonight."

After she hung up the phone, Jane could feel a ball of tension form in her chest.

Strike one. By the time she'd made it to Eliza's, her cheery morning warmth had all but faded. Instead sat one big lump of stress—it was right there. In the middle of her chest. If she breathed too hard, it clenched her airways until it felt like she couldn't breathe at all. Even her hands were shaking as she attempted to put the key in Eliza's front door.

What if her parents did or said something to scare him off? Suddenly, she had flashbacks of all those horrid first dates during her teen years. There never was a second date. Her parents were just too odd. Her mom would bring out the baby photos and her dad sat silently, cleaning his gun. The total cliché dating ritual. It was her life. She lived it.

She shook her head as she walked into her sister's house. How did Eliza survive Mom's matchmaking? Obviously, she and Will managed just fine, even though Mom had been front and center through most of it. In fact, they returned from that trip with Mom down to Vegas, and their relationship blossomed. They actually came back engaged—or almost engaged. She couldn't remember. Maybe this wouldn't be so bad. Maybe her mother had settled down a bit. She could hope.

Jane pushed all those thoughts away as she watered the plants and tidied up the nearly pristine place. She was putting a drink coaster in the coffee table drawer when she noticed one of Eliza's many notebooks she had stashed away. She pulled it out and found a pen in her purse. Maybe if she made a few lists—like for errands, and groceries, and bills, and reasons why she and Charles would work out— then she'd be less stressed. Jane was visual, and it helped to get her thoughts down coherently. It calmed her to focus on the good and not so much on the bad. Yes, she definitely needed to make a list.

She sat down and opened the notebook, positive Eliza wouldn't miss a page or two from it.

Strike two.

This day was not getting better. On the first page of the notebook, clear as day, was a note written to someone about Jane. She hadn't meant to read it, but she caught her name several times, so she was curious. It didn't take long to see that this wasn't a happy letter. Jane wasn't even sure it who it was addressed to, and she couldn't tell if Eliza was angrier at Will or Charles. It must've been one of those therapeutic-type notes meant to release pent-up feelings. One of those notes that should've been burned after they were written. It revealed a much deeper—no, shallower—secret than anyone had ever told her before.

Jane's heart dropped, and she could feel a deep shadow overwhelm the knot of tension in her chest.

Eliza was defending her, it seemed. It was written months ago in response to a conversation she'd had, or something… It was backwards to get only half the story, but the half she read was awful.

Seriously? Will Darcy thought Jane was only after Charles's money? And all her feelings were an act, because she didn't love him at all? Was Will kidding? Was this some sort of twisted joke? *That* was the real reason Charles bailed on her—not because they'd gotten too close, but because his friend warned him about her. And Charles—the coward—bolted without asking her, clarifying—nothing. Just suddenly gone.

Jane ripped the letter out of the notebook and crumpled it up.

All at once, his departure made so much more sense. Mortification overwhelmed her, and she felt like she was going to be sick.

So it wasn't until her sister found out from Will, and then she came to Jane's defense, that either man realized they might've been wrong?

It was completely insulting. She felt like she'd been slapped in the face, even though now things were fine. Now they knew she wasn't after his money, so Charles finally deemed her worthy again. Anger replaced the sickness, and suddenly, she didn't want to be anywhere near Charles Bingley anymore.

She stormed out of the house and into her car. She was all the way to the I-15 and heading south before she realized what she was doing. She should've turned around and headed back, but she just didn't care. Instead, she drove blindly for some time as she thought about how ridiculous this was. Charles knew her! Charles should've known better! And Will? The whole time he was falling for Eliza, he was concerned about Jane? What kind of nonsense was that? How could he find fault with one sister for growing up with less money, but not the other?

The gall of him!

She didn't know who irritated her more, Charles or Will—but one thing was certain. She was going to need some serious time to process this. All at once, she felt so, so cheap or—or used—or something. She didn't know. She felt unwanted and cared about and … small and insignificant again.

The helplessness, the fury, the pain … it was all back, except the pain was sharper this time, much more noticeable. This time, she finally had the answer that clicked everything into place. This time, she knew the truth. The man she was falling head over heels for was clearly only here because her sister convinced him Jane was okay to date. Seriously?

Didn't her own merits mean anything to anyone? Jane wanted to shout in frustration.

Why couldn't people see the real her? Why couldn't even the man she loved be loyal enough not to not fall for every rumor or observation someone else made? And who would think she was shallow enough only to love a man for his money? Did Charles never think that maybe she enjoyed his company too? His humor, his personality, his likes, his dislikes…? After all her years of not finding the right guy, did he honestly believe she'd only seen him as an object?

Even if things were different, could she trust that they had changed? What if he became paranoid again every time she mentioned money? Who could live like that? Urgh!

She banged her fist against the steering wheel and was shocked when she felt something wet hit the top of her hand. It was then that she realized she was crying. She'd been so angry, she'd hadn't noticed. Wiping at her tears, she drove on.

It had to have been at least an hour or two before the phone began to ring. Jane pulled over into a little town called Nephi and coasted into a gas station. She looked down at the phone—speak of the devil. Charles must be at her house. There was no way she could talk rationally right now. He'd have to pay her to answer—since she needed his money so much! Once the phone stopped ringing, she turned it off.

Taking in her surroundings, she decided to fuel up and stay away for a while. It was time for a real break, anyway. She had a lot to sort out.

Without any clear direction, Jane headed east and came to an even smaller town than Nephi. She didn't catch the name of it, but decided to drive around. It was gorgeous in its snowy all-white state—old Edwardian and Victorian homes with cozy fireplaces added to the ambiance of peace. They had even more snow than Salt Lake. She found a large park and stopped the car as she watched a few children sledding on the nearest hill. Their giggles brought her to the reality that she was very far away from home, but in the next moment, she realized that it didn't matter. This was so much better than home anyway.

This was peace.

She cried then. Great big frustrated tears joined each other down her cheeks. So this was why he wanted to end everything, and this was why he was so willing to do anything he could to "win" her back. Charles felt guilty for thinking so low of her. But honestly—*honestly*—if Eliza hadn't defended her, he'd still feel the same way. She rested her head on the steering wheel. He never would have seen her for who she was. Ever. And that broke her heart most of all.

Why? Why did Charles matter so much, anyway? Why was she even trying to care for a man who only listened to what others thought? Despite his gifts and effort—what did it matter? Wouldn't she rather have someone who stood up for her, someone who missed her, someone who wasn't so willing to judge her?

Was she that hard to love all on her own?

Maybe she didn't deserve to be happy and have true love and marriage and a family and all that. Maybe she just wasn't the type of girl who …

The last thing Jane remembered was that crying gave her a headache, and she really shouldn't do it.

By the time she'd woken up, it was dark and cold, and the children had gone home. In confusion, Jane popped her chair up—she must have laid it back when she was crying—and then screamed when she saw a light in her window.

Then someone knocked, startling her again.

"Ma'am, can you open your window, please?" It looked like a police officer.

Jane started the car, cranked up the heater, and glided the window down. "Sorry."

"Are you all right?" he asked. "I've had some reports that you were out here in the cold. Do you need anything?"

Her head was pounding and her neck was sore, and that light was really, really bright. "No. Sorry. I was thinking and must have dozed off."

"Are you here visiting anyone?"

"Um, no. I just happened upon this town as I was driving from Nephi."

The officer looked concerned. "There are some nice hotels down in Ephraim, or even back in Nephi—if you'd prefer."

How humiliating. She couldn't believe this was actually happening. "No. I'm fine. I'll go ahead and get back on the road. It's time I went home anyway. I'm so sorry. I didn't mean to scare anyone, or worry anyone. But I'm fine now. I'll . . . I'll leave. Thank you for waking me."

"Well, definitely didn't want you freezing out here in your car on a night like tonight."

Jane laughed nervously. "Yeah. Again, I'm sorry." The town must have thought she was crazy.

"No worries. Just checking in on you." He pointed toward the nearest road. "If you go right and follow that road, you'll hit the main street. Then take a left, and you'll be back on your way to Nephi."

"I . . . thank you." She attempted a smile. "I'll head back now."

"Be safe. And watch out for deer." He gave her a small salute and then thumped her car.

Jane took that as her cue to leave—quickly.

By the time she made it home, it was nearly midnight. She pulled into her parking spot and then picked up the phone. Eight missed phone calls from Charles. And seven voicemails as well as several text messages. Nothing like completely scaring the guy.

She scrolled through the worried texts and then quickly shot one off. "Went for a drive. I'm home safe. Please don't call me or try to push anything. Will talk later."

Jane grabbed her coat and purse and headed up the stairs. There, hanging on her doorknob, was a grocery bag disguising a box with six beautiful Fabergé eggs. Six geese-a-laying. He'd done it.

In another world, in another life—like yesterday—she would've gasped over the delicate gold filigree designs. But now . . . now her heart only dropped. How much had this cost him? And more importantly, what did he think of her when she got excited about such expensive gifts?

She sighed as she pushed open her door. The joy was gone.

Now there was only pain, guilt, sorrow, and shame.

CHAPTER NINE

Seven Swans-a-Swimming

At ten the next morning, Jane found a beautiful silver envelope taped to her front door. Inside was a ticket to the Salt Lake City Ballet that night to see none other than *Swan Lake*. The performance started at seven thirty. Scrawled on a note inside of the envelope were the words—

Jane, I don't know what I've done to hurt you. Forgive me. Today is seven swans-a-swimming. Here is your ticket. If you'd rather go alone, I understand—please just text me and I'll leave you alone for the time being. However, if I don't hear from you I'll be the handsome guy in a tux in the seat next to yours. Love, Charles.

P.S. For whatever I've done, I'm so, so sorry.

Jane's heart melted a bit, but then the large lump in her throat came back. There was no magic here anymore. She just couldn't do it. Maybe she was being a little harsh and intense, but the pain was still too real. She needed time.

Her hands shook as she taped the ticket onto the door and then locked it. As she crawled into bed to hide from the world, she typed up a quick text.

Thank you for the lovely gift. Swan Lake has always been a favorite of mine. Please take someone else instead. I left the ticket on the door for you.

A few minutes later, he texted back, *When can we talk? Whatever it is, I'm so, so sorry.*

She replied, *I promise we will discuss this. I promise. I just need time (a few days to process). Please respect my space. And I'm sorry too.*

He didn't text again. Jane was relieved that he didn't. But after an hour passed and he still hadn't, she became worried, or agitated, or something. Whatever it was, it didn't matter. What mattered was that she'd put some distance between them before she did something she would regret. Time heals all wounds. She knew that, and hopefully, after a few days, she'd be able to see his side of things. Maybe. Either way, it was time she let her mother know they wouldn't be over for dinner that night.

CHAPTER TEN
Eight Maids-a-Milking

Charles took the ticket and replaced it with a vase of yellow roses on Jane's doorstep. Grammy loved the ballet, and then spent a good couple of hours afterward at her house giving him sound advice on how to handle women.

"If she says give her space, you give her space!" She slapped the wide armrest of her recliner. "You men try to control everything and then you go and ruin it, but if you'd just listen, you'd know what to do. Now stop pacing like a caged lion and talk to me properly. You're giving me a crick in my neck, looking up at you like that."

"Sorry. I just don't know what's happened, and I'm worried, and I can't seem to sit still long enough to pretend not to be worried."

"Nobody said anything about anyone pretending anything. Now sit."

Charles chuckled and sat down at the end of the couch to her left. "There. Better?"

"Much."

"But what if she's one of those women who says one thing and means another?"

Grammy shook her head. "Oh, good grief. There you go again."

"I mean it. What if this is a test to see if I'll come banging on her door and hold her while she tells me everything and I'm failing miserably?"

She ran a wrinkled hand through her short gray curls. "If you've gone and found yourself one of those girls who are all drama, be done with her now. However, from what I know of Jane, I'd say she isn't anything at all like that. She's frank. She's sensible. She's kind. If she's asking for time, give it to her. The last thing you want to do right now is overwhelm her." She pointed to his agitated knee bouncing in place. "Good grief, boy. Are you trying to pounce on something?"

He grinned and took a deep breath, then straightened his legs and rested his head against the cushions behind him. "No. I'm just . . . I don't want to lose her. And I feel like I am. I already lost her once, and honestly, I can't—I won't go through this again."

"You won't go through what again?"

"Losing her."

Grammy had the audacity to laugh. Hard. When she was through she actually had a real-live coughing fit. "That is the dang funniest thing you've ever said."

Once Charles saw that she was okay, he said, "You know, I'd come over and pound on your back for you, but I think you deserve to suffer a bit for that comment."

She found the remote and tossed it at his shoulder. "Hush, you. You'll make me wake up Grandpa. Besides, it's true, though. You don't know it yet, but you're so besotted that if Jane Bennet wanted to be lost to you, you'd darn well wait for her over and over again until you got her back.

Don't make rash blanket statements like saying you won't go through this again. You will. You will lots of times." She leaned over and waggled her finger. "And if you do things right, you'll be real grateful you did, too."

There was no other person who treated him like Grammy did. He always felt like he was a ten-year-old boy being scolded all over again, but somehow, greatly loved, too. He could never deny the unbelievable love she had for him. He ignored the truth of her statements and instead decided to bring the conversation back to where it had been. "But what if she never wants to see me again? What if whatever happened is so awful that no matter how long I wait, she'll never come back?"

Grammy shrugged. "Then you move on."

Never. "What?" He sat up. "But I don't want to move on."

Her eyes met his, and she looked at him real hard for a moment. "Then you'd better pray she's as forgiving as she seems to be."

"But I don't deserve it. Not really. I've put her through the worst of the worst—I mean, I doubted her loyalty and dropped her and . . . and... I don't deserve anything good from her." He leaned forward and placed his elbows on his knees. "That's what worries me most. She'll realize just how awful I treated her and decide she's worth so much more than that. Because she is, Grammy. She so is."

"Chazz, you're a good man. You have a kind heart. And you've been jaded many times by women who weren't what you thought they were. Yes, you made a mistake with this one, but any woman worth her weight in gold will see the real you. You two have gotten off to a rocky start, but you know what? I think you'll be okay. Stop worrying about what you can't control. Just remember, you really have no idea what's going on with her, and it's okay. Don't jump to conclusions. Just be there. Be there and be willing to listen when she's ready to talk, and she'll appreciate you so much for it. I promise."

He took another deep breath and let it out slowly. "Okay. I'll stop stressing and let things settle on their own." He glanced up. "But what about the other gifts I have for her?"

"Well, give them. Don't stop that. Besides, it lets her see that you're still there and thinking of her."

He nodded. "You're right."

"Charles, someone close to her could've passed on. She might've lost her job at work. You never know what's going on. Give her space. It'll be fine. Let her mourn whatever she's mourning and when she's ready to speak, she said she will—so she will. You have no reason to believe anything else. Nothing has shown that she's walking away from you. This is all crazy talk. Stop. And let it be."

Charles suddenly stood up and kissed her cheek. He needed to think. "Thank you, Grammy. You make everything better."

"Good. Now go get some sleep. I for one am exhausted, and I know you are too."

He chuckled wearily. "Yes, ma'am." He collected his coat and waved his hand as she began to rise. "No, no, stay and watch your late-night shows. I know how much you love them. You don't need to see me to the door. I love you. Thank you." He kissed her cheek once more before letting himself out.

"Stay out of trouble, you rascal!" she hollered after him as the door shut.

Charles rehashed his grandma's advice as he headed home. There was no reason to get worked up about never seeing Jane again, or to feel upset because she wouldn't speak to him. This was Jane's call, not his. He didn't like the idea of waiting, but if that's what Jane needed, then he'd buck up and do it.

The next morning, he collected his basket of eight different locally crafted artisan milk soaps and lotions and set them in a bag outside her door with a note. He wished he could knock and see her—he missed that pretty smile. He hesitated, but Grammy's words began to ring through his head, and common sense prevailed. Charles was amazed at how lonely his heart could feel in the past two days without her. Why was it that it took him doing something stupid before he realized how much in love with Jane he actually was?

CHAPTER ELEVEN
Nine Ladies Dancing

On the ninth day of Christmas, Jane opened her door for a brisk walk around the complex and found an invitation to a masquerade charity ball for that night. The beautiful silver calligraphy made her burst into tears all over again. A ball! Her whole life, she'd wanted to be invited to a ball, and now she was. And . . . and it was for that night. All at once she felt like Cinderella, not allowed to go, except the only one stopping her from going was herself.

For the first time in a couple of days, her heart began to crack, and the tiniest sliver of warmth returned.

She was the one who couldn't forgive Charles for thinking she was only after his money and didn't love him. She was the one who was making her own life miserable—and most likely his too. Clearly, he was still thinking of her—bringing her the gifts of Christmas even though she was being stubborn.

But she *was* right, wasn't she? She should stand her ground, right? Where was Eliza when she needed her most?

Jane walked back into the apartment and shut the door, and as she placed the stunning invite into the envelope again, she noticed Charles's hurried note on the back.

Jane,
I'll be there. Please come. It would mean the world to me. However, if you choose not to, I understand. And know that whatever is going on, I'm thinking of you...
Love,
Charles

Love.

Could a man love her and still think she was a gold digger? No. He couldn't, could he?

She plopped down on the couch and then sat back up again. Wait a minute. Didn't he already have a change of heart? He clearly didn't think she was only after his money or he wouldn't be here. The man was attempting to fix everything. But if she kept treating this as if they were stuck in the past, she'd never see what was really happening now. She was more caught up in her own embarrassed pride than anything else.

This really was just about her own forgiveness toward a man who thought the worst of her, but had since changed.

And then the reality hit once more and her heart grew just that bit warmer.

Everything *was* hinging on Jane. It was all weighing on *her* attitude and forgiveness.

The true question wasn't whether or not she was willing to go to her first ball with him. The real question was, was she willing to forgive and overlook his stupidity? He saw her. He cared about her. And to keep being so stubborn, refusing to see him instead of allowing him to explain himself, was only hurting her more.

Why not speak with him? Why not allow her heart to soften enough to ask him what he was thinking?

But then a sharp pain pricked her heart as the memory of Eliza's letter came back in full force. Jane tried to push the sadness back out, but it was pretty hopeless. The letter still stung.

Okay. Maybe she wasn't willing to talk about it yet. However, that didn't mean she couldn't talk about it tomorrow. If she had time to prepare herself.

Jane walked into her closet and pulled out the dress Eliza had given her. It worked for the dinner, but it would be perfect for the ball too. Even though he'd already seen her in it, it really didn't matter—what mattered would be that she came.

But would she? Did she dare?

She glanced around the room and found the purple-and-black lace mask she'd bought herself for a decoration earlier that year, never believing she'd wear it. She picked it up, her fingers tracing the intricate beadwork and ribbons adorning it. It'd be absolutely perfect. Though it was just an optional masquerade, maybe she'd wear it. Nothing too dramatic. And then gauge his reaction that way.

She attempted a smirk and put the mask on. Then she held the dress up in front of the floor-length mirror in her bedroom. It was totally dramatic. But fun. She bit her lip and twirled from side to side. It was a ball. An honest-to-goodness ball. And with incredible eye makeup and an amazing hairdo, she'd kill it. Maybe for tonight, she would be Cinderella and surprise her almost-prince at the ball.

For the first time in days, she giggled. Yes, this is where she was meant to be. It felt right to go, and it was about time she listened to her heart over her brain anyway.

Charles waited in his car outside Jane's apartment complex for thirty minutes—hoping she'd come out and he could offer her a ride—before driving over to the charity ball without her. His heart ached, and he wondered again for the eightieth time if he was doing the right thing. He wished he could take her dancing. He'd love to hold her close and be together. She didn't have to talk—not one word—if she didn't want to . . . he just missed her.

The charity event would last several hours. Several very boring and lonely hours. Charles sighed as he walked in and presented his invitation. He was welcomed kindly and shown to his table. Curious, he walked around the empty table and read the place cards. He'd been seated by some pretty influential people, though it didn't look like anyone else had arrived as of yet. So he walked over to look at the items listed for auction instead of sitting down.

His $400 tickets had paid for a small hors d'oeuvres buffet table, and then there would be an exquisite five-course meal—that would be added to his tab if he accepted and handed in one of the place cards at the table. Each person had a few place cards to be used for the dinner, and other items available for purchase to help with the charity. These meals were usually a thousand dollars apiece, but Charles rarely bought a meal.

After hosting some of his own events through work— and witnessing firsthand how much the hotel gouged them with their usual 70% per meal fee, he realized it was much better to simply write a check for the amount of the dinner than to pay for some expensive chef's wages and only give three hundred or so to the actual charity.

There were some nice items up for auction. Summer vacations in the Swiss Alps, Spain, France, Hawaii, and even one for three months on the beach in San Diego—that one was tempting. Oh, so tempting. There were also some cruises up for grabs, as well as fine jewelry, electronic gadgets, season tickets to the opera, theater, and even some sports teams. Choice seats at the upcoming Super Bowl and different hotel and ski resort packages. Fine restaurants and salon visits—it even looked like some plastic surgery too. Why were the people he associated with so desperate to change themselves? So much so that now, it was considered a nice prize to win something like plastic surgery at an auction? Sadly, even his own family had fallen for the cosmetic perfection trap too. Disgusted, he shook his head and turned away.

This night was going to be awful. He knew it.

As he made his way to the hors d'oeuvres, he overheard two women gushing over their gowns and jewelry. Their comments, though sweet, came out almost hostile, as if these women had spent years despising each other.

He looked over the array of foods before him, and all at once, his world seemed so shallow, as though it was lost in a sea of impressing and never truly living, where one was always attempting to one up the other. Maybe that was what he loved most about Jane. She seemed able to ground him, make him realize how nice it was to live in the moment. To enjoy the little things around you—like feeding peacocks and cooking in the kitchen, or even helping kids learn to love to read.

As more and more people came in, he kept away from the table as it began to fill up. He wasn't in the mood to exchange pleasantries or improve his business contacts. No. He really wanted to be anywhere else.

After another hour or so, the dancing began. Couples drifted onto the dance floor, and they focused on the people they'd come with. Once the table was empty, Charles walked over to it and sat down. This really wasn't the sort of place a man came to alone. Why was he here? He should write out his customary check, thank his hosts, and leave. He'd be much more comfortable without this blasted tux anyway.

Just as he reached into his jacket pocket to pull out his checkbook, he got a glimpse of a beautiful girl in a mask, in a very familiar black dress. Did Jane come, or was he imagining things?

Charles froze and waited until the crowd parted again, his heart beating rapidly. Yes, it was Jane. It had to be. There was only one woman who could attract such notice as she did. Several people turned and stared at her as she slowly made her way toward the tables. She was clearly looking for him through that incredibly tempting mask. Her neck craned this way and that, trying to spy him among the dancers. Did she really believe he'd be out there?

Charles stood and made his way over to the buffet table again. He purposely hid behind a cluster of older men hashing out business of some sort. As Jane walked into the back section of the ballroom toward the tables, he saw her skimming each one. From his vantage point, he admired the way the dress swayed with her as she walked. Never noticing him, she passed right by the men—who'd stopped to stare—and then she made her way farther into the dining area.

Charles fetched a drink from the table, stepped up behind her, and whispered, "Hello, fair lady. Fancy meeting you here tonight."

Jane shivered slightly and then turned toward him. Those incredible exotic eyes met his, and he was certain she'd never looked more striking than she did right then. "Thank you for coming," he said.

"How long did it take you to recognize me?"

He chuckled and handed the drink to her. "Are you hiding? As soon as I saw you, I knew."

She glanced down and nodded, and then her eyes met his again. She was here. She was really here. And he knew they'd be okay. No matter what else the world threw at them, they'd make it. "Would you care to dance?"

Her lips formed a delightful smile. "Of course. It's why I came."

"I've missed you."

She glanced away and then met his gaze again. "I've missed you too."

Every single breath seemed to matter. "Let's not talk yet. Let's just enjoy ourselves. And when you're ready, you can tell me everything. Does that work? Or would you rather go ahead and talk? We can find a quiet corner and—"

Jane leaned over and stopped him with a long kiss on the cheek. His collar felt tighter and his breathing much more rapid as her faint perfume mingled with the warm breath on his jaw. Not one to miss an opportunity, Charles wrapped his arms around her, gently grasping her hand and then pulling her in so her sweet breath never stopped tickling his neck. Jane melted into him, her head resting perfectly on his shoulder—one feather from her mask tickling his brow—and ever so slowly, he began to rock with the music.

This was heaven. This was where he was always meant to be. And now that she was here, there was no way he'd ever let her go.

* * *

Jane released a long, giddy breath as she said good-bye to Charles after the ball. It was perfect—even better than she could imagine—and he was the perfect gentleman. He gave her space, never once questioning her motives over the last couple of days, and kept things lighthearted and fun. It was as if he was gently reminding her of everything she'd been missing. If that was his ploy, it worked. Without the heavy discussions, there were plenty of moments to enjoy and be in the moment.

Jane had forgotten how comfortable she was around him. How easily they slid into playful banter. Deep down, there was a strong friendship there. They could easily talk for hours about absolutely nothing. That night, they had—and danced and laughed and got outbid over and over again by some pretty high fliers. But none of it mattered—what mattered was that they were together, and she was allowing her heart to be sewn back together again stitch by stitch.

As they approached her apartment and he walked her to the door, her spine tingled from the light touch of his hand on the hollow of her back under her coat. So warm, so protective.

Charles tugged slightly and turned her toward him. "I have a gift to give you tomorrow. Will you be here?"

She grinned and looked up at him coyly through her lashes—her mask had been removed hours before. "Maybe."

His eyes stared into hers for a little while, then roamed over her features—she loved seeing him smile. "I'll take my chances."

"I bet you've got something fun planned up your sleeve for ten leaping lords."

"Of course I do. However, if you've rather have a night in and catch up, we could do that too. It's up to you."

It was up to her. It was such a simple concept, it amazed her how profound it seemed. All of the joy or sadness depended on her. "When were you planning to come over?"

He shrugged. "The gift is best opened during the evening, so I figured I'd start there. Well, I wasn't sure if I would be seeing you tonight, so honestly, the plans I had were more like dropping the gift at your door again."

She tried not to feel ashamed, but she did. A little. It was time they actually cleared the air. "Would you like to come over for brunch and stay awhile?"

"Are you sure you want me?"

He looked so handsome in his tux, trying to appear nonchalant and not too eager for her answer. It was charming, really. "I think we should talk."

Charles straightened and cleared his throat. "Uh-oh, that sounds a bit ominous."

She tilted her head and swung the mask around her hand. "I don't know if it's ominous, but I think I'm finally ready to explain myself. So, does tomorrow work?"

He nodded, his eyes going a bit serious. "Thank you." Then he unexpectedly stepped forward and placed a soft kiss on her lips and then another. "Thank you for coming tonight. You stole the show—everyone was definitely looking at you."

Oh, good grief. She blushed and went to pull away, but he caught her elbow and tugged her in for another kiss.

This one was a bit more wonderful than the last two. His free hand came up to her shoulder and then cradled her head. Jane was completely lost.

Charles suddenly pulled back.

"Are you okay? Did I...?" She trailed off, not sure what to say.

He seemed to be having a hard time breathing. "No. I mean, yes, I'm okay. I'm more than okay. You . . . uh, you . . ." He cleared his throat. "I forgot how well you kissed."

Jane could feel herself going bright red, and she bit her lip before she said something stupid.

"Don't look at me like that." He shook his head and then grinned. "I want to push open this door right now and never leave."

It sounded like heaven to her. What would it be like to be married to him?

"But we've still got some things to sort out, so I'll see you tomorrow."

She didn't move, and neither did he.

"I mean it. I'm going to walk away right now."

Jane's grin grew.

"Those lips are incredibly tempting. Are you trying to kill my resolve here?"

Yes. "No." She blushed. "Go home, and I'll see you tomorrow."

Neither moved.

Then all at once, he pulled her in. "Just one more for the road."

CHAPTER TWELVE
Ten Lords-a-Leaping

Charles showed up bright and early at eleven the next morning. Thank goodness it wasn't any earlier. After being up so late the night before, Jane had only just woken up when he knocked on the door. She answered it with a yawn. "Hello there."

"Howdy!" He didn't even hesitate, or ask, or anything. She was greeted with a friendly kiss as he brushed past, his arms loaded full of goodies. He was completely light and cheery. Jane wouldn't have been surprised if he'd started to whistle. She followed him into the kitchen, where he dumped everything on the table.

"What's going to happen when we go back to normal and you stop spoiling me all the time?"

He laughed. "Who says anything is going back to normal? I'm loving this way too much."

A tinge of guilt flashed through her. It really was odd to be given so much stuff. But he was happy, and a small part of her loved that doing this brought out the little boy in him. It was so fun to see him like this.

"So, are you going to see what I brought?" He waved her over. "Come here and see."

Jane peeked into one bag and saw a ton of veggies and eggs. "Omelets?" she asked.

"Or a quiche. You get to decide."

"Quiche? I don't think I've ever had a bell pepper in a quiche before."

"Then you've never lived! A southwestern quiche is amazing. That's it, we're making one. Now hurry and look at the rest so I can start."

"So demanding." She grinned and peeked into the second bag. Confused, she pulled out an envelope.

"Ten lords-a-leaping!" He seemed so proud of himself.

"But . . . ?" She opened it up and then laughed. There were two tickets to see a Utah Jazz basketball game. "Clever. There will definitely be men leaping all over the place." He really was ingenious. "I never would have come up with this idea if I had years to think about it."

Charles wrapped an arm around her shoulder. "Stick with me, kid, and maybe I'll begin to rub off on you."

She touched her hair. "I don't know. I'm not sure I'd want my head to grow as big as yours. I like my hats!"

"Hey! Now, get out of my way. I've got a masterpiece to prepare."

"Fine. I'm going to get ready for the day. Tell me when it's safe to come out again."

By the time Jane stepped out of the shower, the place smelled amazing. When she was dressed and came out of her room, the quiche was cooling on the stovetop. "It looks wonderful." She lightly touched the top. It sprang back perfectly. "I have to say, I'm impressed. After the last time you used my kitchen, I wasn't sure you'd be able to pull it off, but this is better than anything I've ever attempted before."

"Don't get too excited. Wait till you try it first."

A few minutes later, she was exclaiming all over again. "It's amazing! I could seriously get used to this. So, when did you learn how to cook?"

For the next twenty minutes or so, they gabbed playfully. It was nice—cozy—*good*.

As the afternoon wore on, they took their conversation into the comfortable living room. When the reality of why he had come over couldn't be ignored anymore, Jane leaned back on her side of the couch and broke into the middle of a trivial thing they were discussing, blurting out, "So, about the last few days…"

Charles imitated her and leaned back on his side as well. "Yes? I was hoping you'd bring it up, but I didn't want to pry."

She decided to test the waters first. "Do you have any idea why I sort of flipped?"

"No. I'm worried that it has something to do with me, but I'm not sure, so until I know, I've promised myself I won't freak out."

Jane took a deep breath and ran her fingers through her hair. "Well, it *is* about you. It's something you did."

"Okay." He shifted uneasily in his seat. "Now I'm sort of freaking. What happened? What did I do?"

She looked down and fiddled with her hands a moment, attempting to stall while she regained her voice. "I found a note written by Eliza when I was at her house the other day."

He looked surprised. "A note for me?"

She shrugged. "I couldn't tell. Maybe you, maybe Will. It had been written a while ago. I'm thinking a few months, at least. And from what I could tell, it wasn't really a note-

note—more like a therapeutic letter defending me and telling you or Will off."

"Oh." Charles leaned forward with his head down. "It was about what happened eight months ago, wasn't it? I can explain."

She crossed one leg over the other. "Please do. I've wondered what I could have done to make you believe me instead of Will Darcy when he told you I was only after your money. And then the other half of me is stunned and very uncomfortable with the fact that you're spending so much on me now—as if I'd somehow given you the impression this is the only way to my heart."

His jaw dropped. "Okay. I didn't see that last part coming at all. You have to realize that yes—I was a fool. I did believe Will. Which is all my fault, not his. If I'd been the man you were expecting, I would've told Will off for even saying something like that, but instead, I took off. Why? That's been the biggest question for me—why would I leave you?

"The answer came to me a week or so ago, and I mentioned it before. I was scared stiff of where we were heading and how much I was falling for you. So I took the first opportunity to run." His eyes met Jane's. "Honestly, I've been miserable without you. It might seem like I'm this guy who's had a ton of experience with women, but not with anyone real in my life. In fact, it's all been from women who wanted my money—my lifestyle. I'm pretty much clueless on how to act around a woman—a real one I love."

"Love. *Do* you actually love me, Charles Bingley?" She didn't know where that question had come from or where she'd got the gall to ask it, but suddenly, she wanted to take it back. Immediately.

"Yes. Oh, I know I do. I've already told you—though I don't think you believed me. I did eight months ago, too—before I left. "

She chuckled and tried to lighten the mood, hoping to hide that her heart was thumping wildly. "No pressure there."

"None at all." He clasped his hands together and leaned his elbows on his knees. "I know I've messed up. I know I've got a slim chance here to get you back. And I know it's all my fault." He rubbed his eyes and glanced back at her. "When Will told me the truth and that he'd been wrong, I felt like such a jerk. I felt such relief too—but like the biggest loser as well. I couldn't imagine you'd ever have anything to do with me again. I half expected you to have moved on already, and I knew it'd serve me right."

"It hurt, Charles. It hurt to believe you'd think that of me. And not just think it, but flee without a second thought."

"You're wrong." He scooted closer. "There wasn't a day I didn't think of you. And miss you. I'd nearly convinced myself to come back and marry you anyway—who cared if you wanted my money? At least we'd be together."

"But I didn't want it! I don't want it!"

He held out his hands. "I know that. I know that for sure now. I know, I know…" He gestured to the room. "And this—all of this Christmas stuff was a desperate plan from a desperate guy to win you back. Not once has the cost of it even entered my mind."

"Not once?" How rich was he, anyway? How could he not have some sort of budget planned for this? It was baffling to imagine.

"And then, after Grammy spent a good couple of hours chewing me out over my actions at the wedding, I knew I had to do something more than usual—something a bit outrageous to show you I was serious. I'm sorry."

"I didn't realize she told you off for two hours."

He nodded. "I did warn you I was clueless about how to treat women, didn't I?"

She shook her head and attempted a smile. "I'm sorry too. I think of all those wasted months when we could've been happier, and I just shake my head. I'm not sure why you'd risk all we had going for a rumor someone else spread. You never came to me—we never talked it out. You just broke up and left me shattered. I grieved way too long for you."

"No. Please, stop." He scooted in even closer and wrapped his arms around her. "I'm sorry. I don't expect you to forgive me, or even understand why I hurt you. I don't. But I understand if you never will."

Jane snuggled against his broad chest and brought her fingers up to play with his collar. From this angle, she felt so small and so protected.

Charles began to play with her hair, lifting the strands and smoothing them back out again, sending tingles up and down her spine. "I don't deserve you," he whispered. "I've never had a relationship like this. I've grown into what I should've been months ago, but how could you believe me? It's too late."

"You're not too late," she whispered, wrapping one of her arms around his back. "I do forgive you. My only fear is that you'll see something else you don't like in me and run again."

"No."

"And so I'm hesitant to commit. I'm afraid of being rejected again." She leaned up and kissed his jaw. "But I do want this. I want this to be real more than anything. You make me so happy. Even without the gifts, you, just you is all I've ever wanted."

"Jane?"

"Mmm?"

"Why are you so perfect?"

Her fingers stopped fiddling with his collar, and a slightly evil streak went through her. She grinned and answered, "Well, someone had to balance your stupidity."

"What?"

Then a great ruckus began. They played and laughed and teased and wrestled and proved once again how perfectly imperfect they both were, and how much they'd each needed such a silly release. It wasn't until much later when Charles had lifted Jane over one shoulder and a neighbor came knocking asking for quiet that the two decided perhaps they should prepare for the basketball game instead. Composed, overheated, and attempting to giggle silently, they walked out of the apartment and down to his car—with a few stolen kisses in between. The last thing Jane remembered Charles asking before he closed her passenger door was, "That was a workout. I'm starving. How about you?" It was then as he winked and ran around to the driver's side that her heart completely flip-flopped over his gorgeous smile, and she realized once and for all that she'd met her match.

And if he were to ask her that moment to marry him, she'd neither hesitate nor wait—she'd insist they'd elope. All this time they could've already been together, why would she ever want him gone?

CHAPTER THIRTEEN

Eleven Pipers Piping

Jane had to go back to work that morning. Charles tried not to miss her too much, but dang it, he did. He'd almost shown up at the school and become the librarian's helper just so they could spend more time together, but he decided not to. Besides, he had a fun evening planned and didn't want to spoil the surprise, so he drove over to his grandma's house instead.

"And how is everything going?" Grammy asked as she opened the door. "Better?"

"So much better." Charles tapped snow off his boots and then glanced around. "Where's your shovel? Let me get this walk cleared for you. Looks like your place got even more snow than mine last night."

"Oh! Would you please?" She turned from the door. "It's in the garage. Let me get my coat and I'll come help."

He shook his head. The stubborn woman. "Grammy, the whole point of me shoveling is so you don't have to."

She gasped and looked back at him. "But how else am I supposed to learn all the gossip?"

Charles tried unsuccessfully to hide his laugh as he leaned over and kissed her wrinkled cheek. "I love you. Now get me a plate of some of those cookies I know you've got in your tin and some cocoa, and I'll be in to answer whatever questions you may have."

Her eyes twinkled. "You promise?"

"Cross my heart."

In a matter of minutes Charles was folding himself into her soft couch and balancing a very full plate full of cookies and sandwiches and any other leftovers she could foist upon him, as well as a large mug brimming full of the hot cocoa he'd asked for. "You didn't have to give me all of this." He sipped from the mug and set it down on a coaster on the small table nearest him.

"After all these years, I know what you really mean when you say you want some cookies." Grammy wagged her finger as she came into the room. "So don't go on pretending you're not starving to death. I know better."

His eyebrows rose, but he bit his tongue. Sometimes he thought Grammy got him confused with his fifteen-year-old self and never really saw that he'd grown up. Nevertheless, the food looked wonderful, and he *was* nearly starving, and so without any more complaints, he dug in. "Thank you."

"Good." She clasped her hands together as she sat down on the chair. "Now tell me everything. What's your gift for tonight? It's the eleven pipers piping?"

"Yes," he said around a mouthful of food.

"So are you still planning on the symphony?"

When he nodded while sipping some cocoa, she broke out in glee.

"Oh, Jane will love that so much! Chazz, she has needed you—that girl is something just special. And I'm so glad you're back to talking again." Grammy shifted in her seat. "So how did you do it? What happened? You promised. Now spill!"

As they walked into the symphony and Charles watched several men eye his lovely Jane—wearing the silver dress from her sister's wedding—his chest expanded another five or six inches. *Yes, she's mine. Yes, I'm that lucky. No, you can't have her—I saw her first.*

It wasn't just the dress that caught people's attention. It was her joy at being at a symphony, that special something that literally drew people to her.

He'd scored excellent seats in the third row. Once the symphony began, Charles couldn't keep his eyes off Jane. With each squeeze of her hand in his, he knew she'd unconsciously given herself away again. She loved every moment, and that joy resonated through her fingers in his.

He leaned over and whispered in her ear, "I love you."

Their eyes met, and she searched his before answering, "I believe you."

But it wasn't conceited, it wasn't prideful or boastful— it was the exact response he'd been praying for this whole time. It was a calm, reassuring, solid conviction. She knew without a doubt that he loved her. She knew it. His breath caught in his throat as her gaze bore into him.

"Thank you for loving me," she said as the applause around them boomed. Then her lips moved in closer, her hand tightened in his, and his breathing stuttered to a stop. "My heart is yours. I've never loved anyone but you."

Later that night as they cuddled together on her sofa, dreaming of their future, he was reminded again just how incredible she was.

"So I've been thinking," Jane said as she snuggled in next to his heart.

"Yes?"

"If we were ever to get married, where would we live?"

"Oh, we're getting married. There's no 'if' about it."

His heart warmed as she giggled. The wisps of her hair tickled his lips and stuck to the slight stubble on his chin. "Okay. I like that answer, but are you planning on staying in New York?"

Oh. He hadn't thought that far in advance. "I'm contracted to work there for the next four months, and then I guess it'll depend on where I'd like to go from there. Where would you like to live?"

"School gets out in May, and then I guess I have no other obligations—though I do love working with the children. However, I'll be happy anywhere."

"There are children everywhere."

"This is true."

"Jane," he whispered against her brow. "You are the one who gets to choose. I left you once, and I'm not going to leave you again. If you would like to live in New York and see the sights, I believe we'd be happy. Traveling home isn't an issue. We can head back whenever you're homesick, or for family functions, or whatever."

"But to see New York, really see it, and not just visit. What an experience." Her voice grew more excited as she spoke.

"It's definitely an iconic and unique place. And it'd be completely bearable if you were there with me to explore it."

She sat up and looked at him. "What if—I know this is crazy talk—but what if we renewed your contract for a year and just had an adventure? Away from family and friends and all of that. To really give us a good start. They say the first year of marriage is the hardest, so let's make certain we have only each other to rely on. That way, we're not caught up in anything but making our own way together."

"And what if we love New York and decide we'd like to stay there forever and have children there and—"

"How many kids do you want? Do you really want children?" Her grin captivated him—and her eyes! They sparkled.

If just the mention of children made her this happy, how could he ever dream of dampening that? "Of course I want kids. How else will my mother's curse come into effect? She always warned me I'd have children just like me when I grew up."

"Oh, no!" Jane chuckled. "Maybe I should rethink this whole kid thing. I don't think I could handle an adorable Charles mini-me running around."

"Think of the mischief," he teased.

"Exactly."

"I love you."

"I really don't care where we live, or how many children we have—as long as we have a few."

"A few?" He pretended to be shocked and push her away, but he instantly brought her back down to his chest again. "How many is a few again? Two? Three?"

"Four, five." She grinned and wrapped her arms around him. "Does it matter?"

He pretended to cough, but then grew serious. "With you, I don't think it would ever matter. You're the one who carries them. I'll be grateful for whatever you'd like to have. And think of how happy our parents will be."

She sighed and squeezed him. "Thank you." And then for no apparent reason, she seemed to remember something. "Oh, dear. I forgot."

"What?"

Jane sat up, looking worried.

"Are you okay?"

"Yes, but I'm not sure you will be."

"Why?"

"Because I totally forgot—I texted her the other day and postponed it, but it's pretty much inevitable. My mom wants you over for dinner."

CHAPTER FOURTEEN
Twelve Drummers Drumming

Jane was relieved to see Charles laugh. "That's awesome. I'd love to hang out with your parents, and eventually, I'll have to introduce you to mine too."

A small shot of anxiety zipped through her. "Wow. This is really happening, isn't it?"

"I hope so," he said.

"Well, I guess if you can survive my family, I'll love yours."

They continued to talk a little longer until Charles's phone alarm went off. "It's time. It's midnight."

"Is something supposed to happen?"

"Yep. It's the twelfth day of Christmas. Come here and get your present." He held his arms out, and she gladly snuggled back into him.

"Mmm… I think this is my favorite gift so far."

He reached over and collected the blanket on the chair next to them, then gently placed it over her. Then he quietly said, "Do you hear that?"

She nestled her head right on his chest. "The only thing I hear right now is your heart." Its deep thud, thud calmed her.

"That's exactly what I'm talking about. Listen to it."

"Boom-boom. Boom-boom." She lightly tapped two fingers against his chest in rhythm. "Boom-boom. Boom-boom."

"I was going to get you tickets to see the Blue Man Group when they come in February. I figured that would be the most fun drumming performance we could see. I was even planning to fly back over from New York just for the date."

"Sounds fun."

"Well, we could still do it if you'd like. But for now, I've found another drum for you."

"Your heart?"

"Exactly. Listen to those beats. They're for you. Every single one. I love you, Jane Bennet, and I promise to care for you, and be there for you, and be your voice of reason—just like you're mine. I promise to shelter you, laugh with you, play with you, and hold you when life gets rough. Will you marry me, Jane? Will you marry me and prove that forgiveness is the greatest gift man could receive?"

Boom-boom. Boom-boom. This was what this felt like. This was security. No big lights or wild proposals in front of everyone. This was a man asking the woman he loved to marry him quietly and alone. Boom-boom. She slowly raised her head from the gentle reminder of his heart and met his gaze. "Yes."

He scooped her up and kissed her then. Long and tingly and perfectly.

"This is definitely my most favorite gift yet."

Charles laughed. "I would hope so!"

Later that day after they went ring shopping at a few places—without any luck—Jane pulled out her present to Charles. "It's pretty silly and meaningless after all of the last twelve days, but here it is anyway."

She watched a bit ruefully as he opened the forest green handmade scarf and hat that she'd worked hours on. Why hadn't she given him something better? She'd had all those days to buy him a better gift—why hadn't she?

"Did you make this?"

"Yes." A hundred things would have been a better choice.

"Are you kidding me? This is so cool! I love it. Not only are you beautiful and smart, but you're talented too." He wrapped the scarf around his neck. "I haven't had a nice thick scarf like this for years. Not since my grammy made them for me when I was a boy."

She flushed, still embarrassed. "Really?"

He put on the hat and modeled it for her. "Aren't I the most dashing man you've seen all day?"

He did. He was so good-looking, her heart somersaulted. "Yes."

"How did you know green was my favorite color?"

She didn't remind him that she'd known for months now. Instead, she grinned at his profile and felt her heart lift and warm as she studied how good the gift looked on him. "It suits you better than I thought it would."

"Do you know why?" His eyes sparkled into hers.

"Why?"

"Because I'm so hot."

She rolled her eyes and pushed him away. "You're probably really hot in that scarf."

"Come kiss me and see for yourself."

* * *

"Hello, Mrs. Bennet." Charles offered his hand and was crushed into a hug instead.

"Welcome! My, isn't this such a fun surprise?" The woman gasped and then squealed as she moved past him and hugged Jane. "Eeeh! I can't believe it. Both of my girls, married! It's just so exciting! And to such handsome, wonderful men!"

Jane laughed and attempted to pull out of her mom's strong embrace. "We're not married yet."

Mrs. Bennet clasped her hands together. "I know! But soon. And think of how fun it'll be to plan another wedding. I can't wait to call all of the family!"

Mr. Bennet leaned over and held his hand out for Charles. "Welcome to the family, son. It's good to have you."

Jane walked toward the kitchen. "I thought you would've told all the family by now. I mean, I let you know three hours ago."

"Ha! I meant all of the *rest* of the family."

Charles and Jane's dad followed them into the nice eat-in country-style kitchen.

"But I need to warn you, Mom." Jane put her hand on her mom's shoulder. "I really don't want a huge wedding. Charles and I have talked about inviting maybe fifty people or so. Nothing like Eliza and Will's guest list of five hundred. It was ridiculous."

"You know what's ridiculous? Believing we can actually pull off a wedding thinking we could only invite fifty people and not offend the rest. And then there's Charles's family too. He'll want to invite people."

"Mom."

"What?"

110

Charles sat down in the nearest chair he could find. "Mrs. Bennet, this smells amazing. Jane is lucky to have such a great cook for her mom."

Thankfully, Mr. Bennet took the hint and sat down too. "It does smell good, hon. Are you two going to keep arguing, or will we actually get something to eat before it gets cold?"

The older woman waved her hands and shooed Jane to a seat. "Gah. You've got me all flustered. Now sit down. Let's say grace and enjoy some of this grub. Your dad needs to eat or he'll start getting grouchy."

"This is true." He leaned back and patted his stomach. "If I don't get fed, ain't no one happy."

Jane smiled weakly over at Charles as if to say, *Sorry. This is my life.*

But he just shook his head and grinned. Honestly, she'd never met his family. He had at least seen hers from time to time at business events through Eliza. But poor Jane—she had no idea what she was in for. His family... now, his family was a bunch of—well, snobs, to put it nicely.

Except Anne. His little sister Anne was amazing. But with Caroline and Olivia and his parents' crazy attempts at cosmetic perfection, yeah, he was grateful to have at least this bit of normalcy in his life.

When Charles thought about it, he knew they'd never approve of Jane, but it didn't matter. He wasn't marrying the love of his life to please his family—he was doing it for himself.

For the first time in his life, he wasn't going to wait to hear what someone else had to say—he was going to do what he knew was best. And heaven help anyone who thought they knew him, or knew Jane better than he did.

He'd already learned that lesson, and he wasn't ever going to give her up again.

The End

My Persuasion

CHAPTER ONE:

Caroline Bingley walked into the store, mumbling under her breath as she brushed aside her blonde hair. Today of all days would be when the darn curly lock refused to stay in place. How many bobby pins had she already used on the thing?

After flipping on the lights, she set her purse on the back counter and rummaged inside to find another bobby pin and her comb. Thank goodness the store wouldn't open for another hour or so. At least she'd have a few minutes to compose herself before she needed to begin restocking the shelves.

She could tell it was going to be one of those mornings, and she had no one else to blame but herself. With a sigh of relief, she found both the comb and the hair pin—the way the day was going, it looked to be touch-and-go for a minute there.

In the small bathroom at the back of the store, she took one glance at the frazzled mess that was supposed to be hair and groaned. It was literally a disaster. She rarely had bad hair days, which made this one all the more frustrating. She never should have taken the phone call. Not only had she spilled orange juice all over her favorite top, but the other ones that matched her pants were being washed as well, so she'd had to rethink and change her entire outfit. Down to the jewelry, too.

Now the hair had to go. It just had to. Without her curling iron or nice brush, she whipped out every bobby pin she could find and then attempted to use the small comb to repair the damage. Could she actually get away with a ponytail today? If the clothing store wasn't Contessa, only the highest-end clothing boutique in Salt Lake City, she might not have worried too much. However, everything about her appearance mattered. Always. If she didn't look like a Contessa girl, and like she belonged in that world, no one would buy a thing.

After a few more minutes of arranging and then rearranging, Caroline finally settled on a Bohemian braid. It wasn't the intricate bun or the sleek, understated chignon she usually went for, but the braid was chic, and pretty enough to pass muster. She double-checked her outfit and then went to work.

Why, oh why, had no one thought to warn her that Mr. Danning was flying in from New York until this morning? She glanced at the slim silver watch at her wrist and then began to open the boxes of inventory that had come in last night. The same three boxes that were over a week late, due to a mishap with the shipping labels. Really? *Really?* They had to be late now?

She had just forty minutes to process each item of clothing into the computer and then display them on the racks with the instructions provided. Most stores had three days to complete the setup. Caroline took a deep breath and began scanning the first box of clothing. Nothing would get done if all she did was worry about it. So what if Mr. Danning saw the place in complete disarray? What's the worst thing that could happen?

She'd be fired in an instant. Good-bye, management position—hello, poverty again. Ha. Okay, so she'd never really been *broke*-broke, but it was close, which was a far cry from a few years ago, before the recession, when her family was on the top of the store chains. They owned several prestigious clothing stores—all of which folded, or were sold. She was expected to climb into the CEO chair eventually, but that all ended when her father was forced to retire early due to low sales. Now, instead of sitting at the top of the business world, she worked her own store and made a much more meager salary.

After about ten minutes, Caroline heard the doorbell announcing that someone had just come in through the back. "Janice? Is that you? Mr. Danning will be here today, and we *just* got the boxes that were lost in shipment to be processed and displayed. I'm trying not to freak out. I'm so glad you came early."

Caroline finished one pile of clothes and opened the plastic covering of the next—new lilac-colored blouses. As soon as she felt Janice approach from behind her, she reached into the box and handed up another pile of plastic-covered clothes. "Can you work on scanning these so I can get this display set up and steamed?"

No one took the package she held. She glanced up, and her jaw dropped. "You're not Janice." There stood a man she was certain she'd never see again. "Frederick! What are you doing here?"

He seemed just as stunned as she was. "I own this store. What are *you* doing here?"

"But I thought Mr. Danning owned the store."

He looked over the mess. Clothing stacked on chairs, plastic wrap, boxes—she wanted to die. "No, Mr. Danning inspects the stores for me. He'll be here later."

Why would Frederick Wentworth own the place? Did he even like fashion? "Oh. I had no idea."

"I had no idea *you* worked for me."

She wished she could quit right then. "So you're in town and came by to check on the store?"

He cleared his throat and shrugged. "I moved back."

Caroline didn't have a clue what was happening, but very slowly, the small back room began to shift and everything got a bit fuzzy. She put the unopened package back in the box and then tried to get up. Bad idea. Very bad idea.

One moment she was up, and the next, she was falling into the arms of the man who hated her more than anyone. The guy she rejected seven years ago.

Dear Reader,

As I embarked on this new and adventurous journey of writing Regency romance, I wanted to create a series that would showcase my love of England and the joys I've felt while imagining her during the Regency period. For this very first book, I've gone out on a limb and chosen a real woman in history, though her name has been changed. She was an heiress, which was rare at the time, and a hidden bluestocking as well. It fascinated me to have a woman be so independent. Hence, the wonderful Lady Lacey Lamb was born, and what I envision her own romance must have been like. I hope you enjoy this new endeavor of mine and escape into a world that leaves you a bit happier and more hopeful than when you started the book.

Love,

Jenni James

The Bluestocking and the Dastardly, Intolerable Scoundrel

Regency Romance

Book 1

CHAPTER ONE:

Lady Lacey Lamb, Viscountess Melbourne, was in high fidgets as she paced indignantly across the intricately woven rug in the library of her newly purchased townhome on Green Street. "Are you certain it was my name the insufferable swines were bandying about?"

She swirled around to face her second gardener, a respectable Mr. Toppens, who had only this moment returned from the errand she had sent him on earlier that morning. The old garden was in shambles, and one could not think when one's garden was in shambles, which is why it was imperative she bring up all of the gardening staff to the new home immediately. Toppens had been to fetch the seedlings she arranged to be picked up and had come back not only with the seedlings, but also with the most hideous piece of shameful gossip that had crossed this threshold yet.

"Yes, my lady. I came directly home soon as I heard." He fidgeted with his hat and stepped from one foot to the other.

"Thunderation!" she grumbled as she spun on her heel again, her brown muslin gown spinning with her. "Abominable. Unspeakable toads."

"Now, calm down," Pantersby, her normally sympathetic butler, attempted to soothe her. "You do not know the whole of it yet. It could be mere gabblemongers having a laugh at your expense."

"My expense! That is what causes me the most ire. No matter how anyone chooses to look at this, it has been done at my expense."

Both men jumped as she flung the small book she had been clutching upon the chiseled table before her.

This would not do. She was not some horrific shrew of a woman who shouted the place down. Placing her hand to her throat, she took a deep breath to calm the roaring of anger in her ears and struggled to ask coolly, her voice shaking a bit unevenly, "Tell me again, Toppens. What precisely did occur outside of White's?"

Toppens glanced anxiously at Pantersby and cleared his throat. "Lord Alistair Compton was in the midst of the throng."

"Are you confident it was him?"

"Yes, my lady. It was his height, standing a good head and shoulders above the rest—could not have been anyone else but he."

She nodded and closed her eyes. "Continue."

"He and a right large group of nobs came out of White's all boisterous and lively like, the whole lot of them laughing up a storm—never heard so much racket in my life. So, as I was waiting for the line of coaches to ease up a bit—seems as though everyone is coming to town today—I looked over and saw them all. And they were loud as crows, they were, shouting to the skies how as their betting at White's would give Lord Compton ten-to-one odds to get you, Lady Icey Lamb, Viscountess Melbourne, to fall dreadfully in love him by the end of the Season."

Apprehension gripped her chest as Lacey took another deep breath. This could not be happening. This simply could not be. "Icey? They think I am made of ice? Merely since I refuse to become a flirtatious chit in their presence? Now, because I declined to stand up with that buffoon Compton at Lady Huffington's ball, they must place wagers as if I were some token to be won? Infuriating villains. How dare they?" Lacey would have found another book to throw, but stopped herself. There was no need to ruin a perfectly magnificent library because of a bunch of nodcocks.

"'Tis why I came straight to you, my lady. I supposed you must know immediately to put this to stops."

"Yes." Her eyes lit up on the older silver-haired man. "Pantersby, is there anything that can be done?"

"Apart from castrating the lot of them?"

Lacey gasped and threw her hand to her mouth to stop the surprised giggle that was attempting this very moment to show itself. "Pantersby! Why, I never!"

He stood prim and proper, his uniform sharp, though one mischievous side of his mouth turned up the merest bit. "Yes, my lady?"

She gave in and a smile broke out, then a chuckle. Pantersby always had a way of helping her find the lighter side of any situation. But this was a larger mess than she had ever been in. Nonplussed, she sat down upon the nearest chair, her brown skirts in a wild array, as she took in the gravity of the situation. "Why can I not have peace?" She sighed. "This is precisely why I cannot abide *le beau monde* or the Season. I loathe coming here. A bunch of false gossipy twits trying to outdo each other in the most repulsive display of the marriage mart. Little gels with their hopeful mamas, wistful to catch the lucky looks of a mere stranger." She let out a very unladylike groan. "It is the most pitiful excuse of an existence there is—and I must endure it year after year."

"Well, if I may be so bold?"

She waved her hand. "Go ahead, Pantersby. You are most welcome to say whatsoever comes to mind, for nothing can be as dreadful as this. And Toppens, you may go. I thank you for the information. Though shocking, I am more grateful to have it than not."

Once the second gardener left, Pantersby continued, "You have two options here." He took a step forward. "You can pack up and run to the country again, as you are usually wont to do—this will force Lord Compton to forfeit his outrageous bet."

"Or?"

"You gird up your armor and stay to commence a battle."

Intrigued, Lacey sat up. "How so?"

"You teach that youth a thing or two about manners, for one. A bluestocking does not become a prestigious bluestocking because she is a simpleton. No, my lady, you have an opportunity to school the brat and set him down a peg or two."

One slim finger thoughtfully tapped her mouth. "I do have the upper hand, thanks to Toppens."

"That you do."

She scrunched her brow. "But I despise petty games like this."

"You can learn to enjoy them, you know."

"I can?" She stood up. There was no reason she should be in sulks over this. "So I can. And I will." She walked over to Pantersby and nodded once before stepping past him into the gallery. "I shall teach this dastardly, intolerable scoundrel the foolishness of placing one's bet before his comrades." A small grin began to form itself upon her features once more as an indignant brow arched. "Society may come and go as they please and attend their silly soirees and galas. I am here for Parliament alone. Women cannot yet attend, but the newspapers are quick in London, and my brother, Lord Melbourne, will continue to tell me the Whig ondits. I will have all the fascinating knowledge I need to entertain myself. However, this need not mean that I should be put out between sessions."

She walked to the center of the vestibule, placed her simple, unadorned bonnet atop her fiery red hair, and tied the bow rakishly to the side. Then she allowed Pantersby to slide her green woolen pelisse about her shoulders. "Please have Jameson bring the curricle around."

"Are you to go out alone, my lady?"

Lacey sighed as she tugged on her kid-leather gloves. "Do you think I ought not?"

"You know very well what I think. 'Tis too dangerous for you to be out and about without Mrs. Crabtree, or a footman at the least."

"If *men* can banter my name willy-nilly all over the place, I see no reason why it is not permissible to grant me the opportunity to defend myself and do the equivalent."

"You are not going to White's! 'Tis a gentleman's club. Please say that you are not."

Lacey closed her eyes and took yet another deep breath. Life was not just, and Pantersby was fortunate that she esteemed him as family or that outburst would have harmed him greatly.

"Begging your pardon, ma'am. I do not know what came over me."

She took her reticule from the same side table where all the rest of the folderols had been and then met his eyes.

"Do not worry. You are only attempting to make me see reason. To remind me of these confounded rules of town. No, I had not one notion to attend White's and place my own wager, making a fool and mockery of Lord Compton. Why should I ever do that?" Lacey tugged forcefully on her pelisse and gestured for Pantersby to open the door for her.

"No, I will allow my brother to avenge my wrongs. And as surely as I speak the truth of the matter to him, he will most certainly place the bet for me, and then Lord Compton and I will be on even ground, no?"

Pantersby gave a smug grin. "No, Lady Lamb. Not one whit of you shall be on even ground with such a man. Indeed, you are, and always will be, scores above him."

"Thank you, Pantersby."

He opened the door to the drudgery of London's finest attempts at weather and sent a footman scurrying to the lady's side to await the curricle.

"And what of the wager? Have you thought of a sufficient reply to his?"

Lacey smiled at the bottom of the steps of her new townhome and said, "Why, it will be to guarantee that he shall tumble topsy-turvy and head over heels in love with the Icey Lady Lamb." She chuckled at Pantersby's face above her. "The best part is, Pantersby, I have enough to my name that I can easily lose the despicable wager. Lord Compton, I believe, is such a wastrel of man, he does not. Either way, he fails, and perhaps next Season, he will learn to be a bit less of a libertine and more of a gentleman. Why, his mama may thank me when this is all through."

About the Author:

Jenni James is the busy mother of ten kids and has over twenty-five published book babies. She's an award-winning, best-selling author who works full-time from home and dreams about magical things and then writes about what she dreams. Some of her works include The Jane Austen Diaries (*Pride & Popularity, Emmalee, Persuaded...*), The Jenni James Faerie Tale Collection (*Cinderella, Snow White, Rumplestiltskin, Beauty and the Beast...*), the Andy & Annie series for children, *Revitalizing Jane: Drowning, My Paranormal Life, Not Cinderella's Type*, and the Austen in Love Series. When she isn't writing up a storm, she's chasing her kids around their new cottage and farm in Fountain Green, entertaining friends at home, or kissing her amazingly hunky hubby. Her life is full of laughter, crazy, and sunshine.

You can follow her on.

Facebook: authorjennijames

Twitter: Jenni_James

Instagram author Jenni James

Amazon Page (follow to get updates when a new book is released): www.amazon.com/Jenni-James

She loves to hear from her readers. You can contact her via—

Email: thejennijames@gmail.com

Snail Mail:

Jenni James

PO Box 449

Fountain Green, UT 84632

Other books by Jenni James:

The Jane Austen Diaries

Pride & Popularity

Persuaded

Emmalee

Mansfield Ranch

Northanger Alibi

Sensible & Sensational

Regency Romance

The Bluestocking and the Dastardly,
Intolerable Scoundrel

Lord Romney's Exquisite Widow

Lord Atten Meets His Match (2017)

Cinderella and the Phantom Prince

Austen in Love

My Pride, His Prejudice

Jane & Bingley

My Persuasion

Modern Fairy Tales

Not Cinderella's Type

Sleeping Beauty: Back to Reality

Beauty IS the Beast

Children's Book:

Andy & Annie: A Ghost Story

Andy & Annie: Greeny Meany

Prince Tennyson

Women's Fiction

Revitalizing Jane: Drowning

Revitalizing Jane: Swimming (2017)

Revitalizing Jane: Crawling (2017)

Jenni James Faerie Tale Collection

Beauty and the Beast

Sleeping Beauty

Rumplestiltskin

Cinderella

Hansel and Gretel

Jack and the Beanstalk

Snow White

The Frog Prince

The Twelve Dancing Princesses

Rapunzel

The Little Mermaid

Peter Pan

Return to Neverland

Caption Hook

Other Books

Princess and the Pea

My Paranormal Life

Made in the USA
Las Vegas, NV
02 December 2020